CLARISSA & THE COWBOY

ALIX NICHOLS

The Darcy Brothers

Find You in Paris

Raphael's Fling

The Perfect Catch

Clarissa and the Cowboy

Game Time

Playing with Fire

Playing for Keeps

Playing Dirty (Fall 2017)

La Bohème

Winter's Gift

What If It's Love?

Falling for Emma

Under My Skin

Amanda's Guide to Love

COPYRIGHT

CLARISSA & THE COWBOY: AN
OPPOSITES-ATTRACT ROMANCE

***Clarissa & the Cowboy is a hot and
hilarious standalone within the Darcy
Brothers series.***

~ **Nathan** ~

Right now Clarissa, our tour guide, is talking about
prehistoric cave paintings.

In a moment, she'll point at the mammoth... Wait
for it....

"Look at the mammoth on your right," she says.

Told ya! I've done her tour six times in two months.

Everyone gawks at the mammoth.

My eyes stay trained on Clarissa's lovely face.

After the tour, I'll ask her out, fully expecting her to
say no.

I mean, why would a hotshot Parisian archeologist go on a date with a dairy farmer from the sticks?
But I need to hear Clarissa's no.
Maybe then I'll be able to forget her.

~ Clarissa ~

Nathan, aka Cowboy, is here again. Staring at me again.
I ignore him.
Just as I've ignored the hot, disturbing dreams I've been having lately.
Dreams in which a handsome cowboy undresses me.
Kisses me.
Pleasures me into oblivion.
Crazy dreams!
In real life, I'm going back to Paris to start a new job in a big museum.
The one thing I don't need during my last week in Burgundy is a roll in the hay with Nathan.
Even if that roll turns out to be better than my craziest dreams...

NATHAN

nne-Chantal gives me a knowing smile and pushes my ticket across the counter. "Here you are."

"Thank you."

My tone is polite and hopefully formal enough to discourage any comments she might be tempted to make.

"The tour starts in five minutes," she says.

I nod and, exhaling a sigh of relief, move to turn away.

"You're *really* into prehistoric cave art these days, aren't you?" she says, tilting her head to the side.

"What's wrong with enjoying—"

"Nathan," she butts in, arching an eyebrow. "This is your fifth tour of the Darcy Grotto since January."

Not that you've been counting or anything, I itch to say, but decide against it.

Anne-Chantal is one of Ma's bosom friends and a frequent guest at the farm. Even though she sometimes boxed my ears when I was a kid, I owe her respect.

Anyway, busybodies are inevitable when you live in a village where everyone knows everyone.

"Fifth, you say?" I feign surprise. "I guess I *am* really into cave art."

With that, I shove the ticket into the pocket of my jeans and march to the area where two dozen visitors are waiting for our guide, Dr. Penelope Muller, to show up and start the tour.

Her scrawny assistant Nina arrives first and delivers her introductory spiel. "It's going to be chilly inside the Grotto. So, if you left your coat or jacket in the car, you might want to go get it now."

Several people dash out.

As before every tour, I can't help wondering if Nina ever eats anything beyond the occasional lettuce leaf. If I wasn't wary of giving her false hope, I'd take her to the farm and make her sample our dairy products.

If Girault cheese and butter don't transform her into a foodie, then nothing will.

"Nathan, hi! You're back." Nina smiles and tucks a strand of hair behind her ear.

We cheek kiss.

Like her boss, Nina isn't a local. But she claims she loves Burgundy with its lush vegetation, gentle rivers, and hills. She also loves country life. And, above all, she loves farm animals. Especially, cows. Nina's most cherished dream? To settle down in the region and become the wife of a dairy farmer.

At least that's what she told me when we bumped into each other about a month ago, in early February, at the opening of the cattle fair in Auxerre.

I asked her if her boss shared her aspirations.

"Clarissa?"

"Um... I thought her first name was Penelope?"

"It is." Nina played with a lock of her hair. "Clarissa is her middle name. She doesn't care for her first name and only uses it professionally."

Clarissa.

I took a moment to adjust my go-to fantasy in which I whisper "Penelope" while pushing hilt deep into her welcoming heat. As sexual fantasies go, this one is as much vanilla as it is a pipe dream. Thing is, I've never been with a woman—let alone someone as refined and far removed from my world as Dr. Muller —who could fully accommodate my length.

I wouldn't call myself a freak of nature, but there's no denying I'm larger than average. A lot larger. My neighbor and friend Celine once suggested I should book an appointment with a specialized surgeon to see if they can "trim" my "thingy" a bit.

"I know a woman who had her breasts reduced from an F cup to B cup, and it changed her life," Celine said.

No way in hell was my answer.

Then she came up with another idea. Why not try full penetration with a professional first? To be honest, I'd toyed with the idea a few years back, but I couldn't bring myself to pay for sex.

"That's because you aren't desperate enough," Celine offered when I rejected her second scheme. "Unlike the average farmer, you never had any trouble getting laid."

My guess is that by "average farmer" she meant herself.

Anyway, when I asked Nina what Clarissa thought of Burgundy, she rolled her eyes. According to her, Dr. Muller will get out of here as fast as lightning the day her research at the Grotto is done.

Of course, she would.

I don't know where Nina gets her romantic notions about country life from, but running a big farm is one of the hardest jobs I can think of.

A cheerful "hello" uttered in the world's most pleasing voice brings me back to the present moment.

Clarissa has arrived, sharp on time.

Dressed in a silky white blouse, black pants, a tailored black jacket and a pretty scarf around her neck, she's as classy as ever. Another friend of mine, Danny, who came along on my third tour, claimed she wasn't beautiful. Then again, Danny's standard for female beauty is Pamela Anderson from *Baywatch*.

Clarissa's breasts are pert little handfuls, nowhere near Pamela's cup range. The tip of her thin high-bridged nose looks down. She wears glasses, very little makeup, and has naturally brown hair.

And yet... to me, she's the sexiest thing alive.

Maybe I have a hand fetish.

Clarissa's delicate, long-fingered hands are out of this world. But they aren't the only thing she has going for her. On my first and fourth visits, she wore a skirt, giving me a chance to see her shapely long legs. Not just see them—study them, caress them with my gaze, and commit their lines to memory.

Then, there's her voice. Its clear, velvety sound makes my heart beat faster. Her intelligent gaze turns my brain to pulp. So much so that I still haven't plucked up the courage to ask her my prepared questions during the tour and ask her out after the tour.

Clarissa's competence and subtle humor leave me in awe.

As for the grace with which she carries herself, it has my cock on speed dial.

"Stop staring. You'll burn a hole through her," Anne-Chantal whispers with an amused smile on her face as she sails past me.

Great.

I can see her calling my mother the moment I'm out of earshot to tell her what she thinks about my *fifth* visit. Blanket denial combined with insinuations that the woman is so bored with her job she sees things that don't exist will be my best line of defense.

Anne-Chantal unlocks the heavy door and ushers everyone in before closing it behind us. I guess the animals painted on these walls are too precious to risk some moron creeping in at night and spraying his own version of a wild beast over them.

"Bone fragments and tools made by the Neanderthal man who lived here some 60,000 years ago were found in the Bison Cave and Hyena Cave," Clarissa explains as we begin the tour.

Having taken it four times already, I know what comes next, even though she does improvise a lot. The group hangs on her every word, staring at the masterfully painted reindeer, mammoths, rhinos, and horses.

"The beautiful Paleolithic art you're looking at," Clarissa says, "is the work of the Cro-Magnon—the modern humans—who moved in here some 40,000 years ago."

As she takes us to the Mammoth Hall, the largest of the interconnected caves, she explains that until two decades ago, no one knew about the existence of the paintings. Tourists came to the Grotto to admire its stalactites, stalagmites, and underground lakes. They were given a piece of stalactite as a souvenir at the end of the visit, and they left unaware that these caves held an extraordinary human-made treasure hidden under a layer of calcite.

As we progress from cave to cave, I keep staring at Clarissa. She doesn't look at me, not once.

All too soon, the tour is over.

Several visitors surround Clarissa to ask their questions.

I hover by the entrance for a few minutes, and then stride out and get into my car. As I drive off, I decide that I should forget about her. It's foolish to expect Dr. Muller, a lady and a scholar, the young and ambitious curator of the Darcy Grotto Museum, to care for a local farmer.

She could also be frigid.

Alternatively, she could be only interested in older men.

Or women.

Or group sex.

And even if I did manage to get under her skirt, what would be the point? I'll give her my heart—she practically has it already—but the moment there's an opening in some fancy museum in Paris or another big city, she'll zoom out of here like a meteor.

Ah, the voice of reason!

Thank you.

I'm giving up.

2

CLARISSA

After dessert, everyone moves to the drawing room, splitting into small groups. The butler serves a selection of sweet wines for ladies, whiskey and eau-de-vie for gentlemen, coffee for me, and a spiced chai tea for the mayor's wife.

Genevieve sits down by my side on the sofa and spends a few moments watching me watch Sebastian and Diane.

"I'm sure he's brought her here with the sole purpose of making you jealous," she says, pointing her chin toward the couple.

Oh, I doubt it.

For the first time in months—make it a year—young Count Sebastian d'Arcy du Grand-Thouars de Saint-Maurice has come to a house party at his family estate in Burgundy with a woman on his arm. And, to make

9

sure there was no doubt in anyone's mind as to her status, he introduced her as "Diane, my girlfriend."

A tomboyish checkout clerk, Diane is nothing like the regal heiress he dated last year. Nor does she have much in common with the overachieving me, or any other woman I've ever seen within flirting distance of Sebastian.

Perhaps that's why he's into her.

Because, he *is* into her.

There's no way the desire in his eyes when he looks at Diane is fake. Besides, why would he bother scheming when he knows he can have me anytime? Nothing has been said between us, but I've dropped enough hints and given him more than enough seductive smiles and glances over the last year.

He *knows*.

And I know that he knows, even if my self-proclaimed friend Genevieve seems to believe I'm a nerd with zero emotional intelligence.

Last time Genevieve and I crossed paths was at Raphael's birthday party here at Chateau d'Arcy. I had too much to drink, which had the unfortunate effect of blunting my instincts and loosening my tongue. Genevieve confessed to me she was in love with the middle d'Arcy brother and her childhood friend, Raphael. I admitted I had the hots for the oldest brother, Sebastian.

"Here's to snagging the two most eligible bachelors in France!" Genevieve raised her glass. "Sebastian is worth a billion, and Raphael isn't far behind."

"It'sh not about his money," I slurred.

"Naturally." She gave me a wink. "I would never imply something so vulgar."

My ears still burn with shame every time I remember that exchange.

Truth is, it *is* a little bit about his money.

Not in the sense that I'm eager to lay my hands on one of the country's oldest and biggest fortunes. Even though I like nice clothes as much as the next woman, I'd rather make enough to buy them myself than latch onto a man with deep pockets.

No, the way money affects my feelings for Sebastian is subtler than that.

Never mind that he owns a huge fragrance company, multiple houses in France and abroad, a Greek island, a private jet, and one of the largest estates in Burgundy. What matters is that said estate includes the Darcy Grotto and the adjacent museum that I curate. And that makes Sebastian the lucky owner of one of the most ancient and remarkable Paleolithic rock-art caves in Europe.

It's as if owning those cave paintings were his personal achievement, as if he'd *created* them or, at least, discovered them himself.

Sebastian is handsome and cultured, albeit aloof. I decided he was very attractive the day I first met him. But I can't help wondering if I'd be just as impressed if he were a local librarian or a mail carrier.

Or a dairy farmer.

I tune back in and realize Genevieve has been talking to Diane. She must have said something mean, because Diane purses her lips and there's a hard look in her eyes as she glances at me.

Wait a second! Why is she looking at me? *What did Genevieve say?*

Panic seizes me as I consider the possibilities.

Apart from inviting me to dinners and house parties at the castle—along with the mayor, his wife, and a bunch of other people—Sebastian has never said or done anything to suggest he was interested in me. What if Genevieve told Diane otherwise? What if she told Diane he and I were seeing each other?

As I sit there, petrified, embarrassment warming my ears and dampening my palms, Sebastian takes Genevieve's place on Diane's right. The next moment, he's kissing her in a way that's too intimate to watch.

That's it, I'm out of here.

Easier said than done.

Sebastian intercepts me before I have a chance to sneak out of the room. He says I should stay, for my safety. He hates the idea of me driving home alone on poorly lit countryside roads.

"You'll sleep at the castle," he announces in a tone which makes it clear the matter is closed.

Next, he calls the housekeeper and asks her to get one of the guest rooms ready.

I mumble thank you and sit down again, not daring to look at anyone—especially, Diane—and bracing myself for more mortification.

Mercifully, Yves Fournier, the mayor of Verlezy, remembers he wanted to discuss something with me. He sits down on my left, his wife Josephine takes the spot on my right, and the three of us spend the rest of the evening plotting how to dovetail the Grotto's outreach with Verlezy Primary's extracurricular activities.

When I finally go to bed, it's one o'clock in the morning.

The emotional shock inflicted by Sebastian and the never-ending discussion with Yves and Josephine have left me drained, which explains why I drop off the moment I shut my eyes. But it doesn't explain the dreams. *One* of the dreams, to be more exact—the one I've been having nearly every night for a couple of months now.

In it, I'm alone in the smallest cave of the Grotto and feeling uncommonly and inexplicably aroused.

The warm flickering glow of several candles lights the room, and there's a musky smell in the air. I lean against the wall and touch myself as I picture *him*. Right on cue, *he* materializes by my side, leans into me, and covers my busy fingers with his large hand. His mouth descends onto mine as he rubs my bud, and I feel a long finger slip inside me.

Oh, oui! Right there. More, please!

He adds another finger and pumps deeper, faster—

I can never remember if he makes me come, but I always—always—wake up wet.

Shocking, I know.

What's even more scandalous is that the man in those dreams is not Count Sebastian d'Arcy. Nor is he one of my five ex-boyfriends. He isn't a faceless stranger conjured up by my imagination, either.

He's *Cowboy*.

Aka the dairy farmer who's taken the tour of the Grotto half a dozen times since January, and whom I often spot at various local events.

I don't know his name.

Since I'd never date him, I'm not even interested in learning it. If ever he tried to hit on me or if a common acquaintance formally introduced us, I'm sure we'd have nothing to say to each other.

For one, he has no interest in archeology.

Whenever I sneak a peek at him during the tour, he's staring at me, not at the paintings on the walls.

And, I don't care for farming.

So, when I find myself in the same room as him, I pretend I don't know who he is. To make my point even clearer, I avoid acknowledging him with a hello or a nod.

He's never on my mind in daytime.

I don't look forward to his next visit or to a chance encounter in the village.

So why those dreams?

NATHAN

My new Workaway volunteer, Lorenzo, points to the trimmed part of the hedge. "How am I doing?"

"Not bad at all!" I nod in appreciation. "You're a natural."

"It's because I've done this before."

I try not to smile as he intones his remark with a singsong Italian accent, adding an "eh" at the end of each word.

"May I?" I take the shears from his hands and clip the little branches that stick out.

Two years ago, Ma planted this hedge around the nicest cottage on the farm after we decided to turn it into a guesthouse for tourists. In spring and summer, they come for fishing and hiking in the area, or just to get away from the city and enjoy some peace and quiet.

I hand the shears back to Lorenzo. "All yours."

The young software engineer from Florence and his girlfriend arrived two days ago, and will stay through May, working four hours a day in exchange for accommodation and food.

When they're gone, I'll take in two new people. The farm has three single-story cottages on its grounds, built by my grandfather and updated with modern amenities by Pop.

I occupy one of them so that Ma and I don't crowd each other's space. The second cottage is for paying guests. The third one—only big enough to serve as temporary lodgings for a single person or a couple— stood empty for years because Ma preferred to put up visiting family and friends in the main house.

So, it made an awful lot of sense to host Workaway helpers in addition to the farmhands we hire when there's too much work.

I should've thought of it myself, but I didn't.

It was Celine's idea. She learned about the program three years ago from a friend, and posted an ad for her organic produce farm the same day. Her first helper was a giggly middle-aged school teacher from Germany. The woman went above and beyond with every task she was given.

Since then, Celine has been hosting a nonstop influx of *Frauen*, with an occasional Dutch or Austrian woman thrown in. All of the ladies fall in love with Burgundy and with Celine's farm. They delight in the food and wine she serves them. Most come back the following year. And some of them fall in love with Celine.

Anyhow, Ma and I decided to give the Workaway thingy a shot, despite our initial skepticism. When milk prices are low and labor costs high, you need to get creative to keep a big dairy farm profitable. Besides, only an idiot would pass up on a highly motivated workforce that's happy with payment in kind and with beautiful landscapes for a bonus.

We welcomed our first volunteers two years ago, and never looked back.

Celine was right to insist.

"Hey, neighbor!" a familiar voice calls.

Speak of the devil.

Celine waves hello as she walks through the gate and gives Lorenzo a bright smile. "Hey, new guy!"

"I'm Lorenzo," he says.

She fist-bumps me and cheek kisses Lorenzo. "My name is Celine. You alone here or with a partner?"

"My girlfriend Paola is inside." He points to the cottage.

Celine turns to me. "Did you talk to her?"

"Paola?"

"No, silly! The *cave woman*."

"Can we discuss that later?" I give Celine a pointed look.

She glances at Lorenzo. "Oh. Sure."

Since we were teenagers, Celine and I have always kept each other updated on our progress—or lack thereof—with the objects of our fixations.

Celine's is rarely a specific person. It's a type. She digs men that are nerdy, skinny, sensitive and preferably bespectacled.

I blame it on Harry Potter and that actor, Romain Duris, both of whom she was hung up on as a teenager. Her more recent crushes—Tim from *The Office* UK, Jim from *The Office* US and Chandler from *Friends*—haven't exactly helped either. I've tried to get her to appreciate guys like Terminator and Rambo by making her watch my favorite 90s action movies, but that was a total waste of time and effort.

Celine may be one tough cookie, but she's hopelessly attracted to men who have less muscle than she does.

I'm not saying there's something wrong with guys like that. Problem is they don't go into farming. While there's no shortage of musclemen among my brothers in plows, you'd be hard pressed to find a skinny nerd.

Come to think of it, you'd be just as hard-pressed to

find stylish, eloquent and graceful female archeologists around here. I'm pretty sure there's just one, and she's afflicted with a strange condition that makes me invisible to her.

It would've been so much easier if Celine and I were attracted to each other!

We'd become lovers and I'd marry my spunky, dependable neighbor who hides a nice body under her checkered shirts and baggy jeans, and comes from a long line of farmers. To top it off, Ma loves Celine with all her heart. We could be very happy together...

But no, the naked guy Eros, God of Horniness, has a sick sense of humor.

My phone lights up with an alert sent to it by the calving sensor in the barn.

"Got to go," I say, standing up. "Gabrielle is in labor."

Celine draws her eyebrows. "You have an alert for that?"

"It's a pretty nifty app," I say with pride, heading to the barn. "Had it installed two weeks ago."

Celine marches next to me. "Could be a false alarm."

"I guess I'll find out."

I pick up the sanitizer, gloves, and wipes from the tool shed and race to the barn.

Celine follows, hot on my heels.

Turns out it isn't a false alarm—Gabrielle is in labor. And, by the looks of her, it won't be an easy one.

I had a feeling this "petite" heifer would have a tough time calving, and unfortunately, I was right. She's fully dilated, her water sac has broken, and the calf has presented as it should—front feet first. But it's too big. And that must be the reason it's stuck in the birth canal.

Looks like a C-section situation to me.

"Time to call the vet," I say to Celine.

"You're sure we can't handle it?" She crouches down and stares, trying to assess the odds. "You and Brigitte managed just fine last time."

Yeah, I wish Ma was here now, but she's on a long-overdue vacation in Provence.

Celine pulls out her phone. "I can snap a pic and send it to her—to get her opinion."

My gaze shifts from Celine to the heifer.

I really don't want to mess this up. Gabrielle and the calf are too valuable to take unnecessary risks.

"We don't need my mother's opinion," I say, all doubt gone from my voice. "We need a vet."

An hour later, it's over.

I have to go fill out a dozen or so forms required by the EU red tape every time a calf is born, but the important thing here is that he *was* born. And he's healthy as is his mother.

"So, how did the Grotto tour go?" Celine asks me when the vet is gone and we've tucked in Gabrielle and the calf.

"Same as last time. Clarissa ignored me so profoundly I lost my nerve."

"You didn't go up to her after the tour?"

I shake my head.

"Did you at least ask your question during the tour?"

"Nope. Didn't have the guts. I'm giving up."

"You're pathetic, Nathan Girault."

I arch an eyebrow. "Says the grown woman with *Harry Potter* posters everywhere in her house."

"Yeah, well, at least I take action. On those rare occasions when I meet a man who fits the bill, I make sure to talk to him, to give him a chance to size me up, and to..." She lets out a heavy sigh.

"What?"

"Let me know he isn't interested."

"So, what's the point?"

"The point is in not giving up. Because you never know."

I shake my head.

"Promise me you'll go back there next week and initiate a verbal exchange," Celine says.

"What for? It's hopeless. I bet that even if I do, she'll just wave me off. I'm too *rustic* for her."

"Then you'll get closure."

Good point. Besides, what do I have to lose?

"One last time, next week," I say. "I promise."

"That's my boy!" Celine gives me a pat on the shoulder and goes home to cook dinner for her *Frau*.

CLARISSA

J ean-Philippe has been the curator of the Museum of Archeology in Paris for at least a decade.

He's been a good friend of my parents for at least twice as long, which is one of the reasons I'd refused his offer to take over as the Paleolithic art curator when the current one retires in a few weeks. All the scandalmongers whispering about nepotism behind my back, staffers citing my family name in hallways, unlucky contenders rolling their eyes as if to say, the old boys are looking after their own... *Grrr!*

If only I could impress upon every single museum curator and archeologist in France that my parents never intervene on my behalf!

But I can't, nor do I believe it would help. Even if I

wore a sign across my chest that said exactly that, chances are nobody would believe me.

Except, it's the truth.

Mother and Father hate owing favors to other people—even to good friends. And they love knowing that my achievements are my own.

As it happens, I love knowing that, too.

Then why am I dialing Jean-Philippe's number at this juncture?

Sebastian d'Arcy, that's why.

True, the count had never overtly flirted with me, but I'd convinced myself flirting just wasn't in his character. I had deluded myself that his interest in the Grotto and his frequent invitations to gatherings at the chateau had meant more than neighborly solicitude and a genuine interest in the rock paintings discovered on his estate.

I was such a fool!

"My dear Penelope, it's so good to hear your voice!" Jean-Philippe says on the other end of the line. "To what do I owe the pleasure?"

I hesitate for a moment and confront the issue head on. "That job you mentioned two weeks ago—is it still up for grabs?"

"I've done a bunch of interviews, but I'm not entirely happy with any of the candidates." There's a brief silence. "Why? Have you had enough of sweet Burgundy and want to move back to Paris?"

"I've changed my mind about the job. It's too good to pass up."

"When I made the offer, you told me you preferred to be a big fish in a small pond rather than a small fish in a big one. I'm just curious—what gives?"

"It's like you said," I lie. "My small pond is beginning to feel like a tiny fish bowl."

"I knew it!" He chuckles, pleased with his perspicacity.

If only he knew how far he is from the truth!

"You were born for the ocean, *mon enfant*," Jean-Philippe says when he's done chuckling. "Your parents have no doubt about it."

My stomach clenches at the brutal accuracy of the latter observation. Jean-Philippe is right. What with being dyed-in-the-wool atheists and certified pessimists, Mother and Father believe in me more than they have ever believed in anything.

And *that* is the root of the problem.

"With the TGV train, Auxerre is less than two hours away from Paris, right?" Jean-Philippe asks.

"That's right."

"So, you can easily zoom to the Grotto, if you need to check something for your research, and be back within the day. Isn't that convenient?"

"It is, indeed."

"Send in your application straightaway," he says. "And expect to be called for an interview very soon."

"Thank you."

"The job is as good as yours, but we'll need to do it by the book."

"You'll be accused of favoritism no matter how we do it," I say.

He chuckles again, unfazed. "Let me worry about that, *mon enfant*."

After I hang up, I email him the application form I'd already filled out, my CV, and a letter of motivation.

That was easy.

If everything goes to plan, I'll hand in my notice in April and move back to Paris. Another archeologist will take over as the curator of the Grotto. As for *this* archeologist, she'll have no reason to cross paths with Sebastian d'Arcy ever again.

My phone beeps, reminding me it's time.

I shut down my computer, grab my jacket, and head over to the cave for the daily tour.

The first thing I notice in the crowd waiting in front of the entrance is the strapping, sun-kissed man who towers above everyone.

Cowboy.

Immediately, I avert my gaze, refusing to acknowledge him and denying him the chance to acknowledge me. It's rude, and God knows I feel guilty doing it, but so far, my selective blindness has worked at keeping him from approaching me.

He hasn't even dared to ask a question!

And that is great on more than just the obvious level of sparing both of us some awkwardness. The second, less obvious and more twisted, level is that I expect him to say something dumb if he opens his mouth. Call me a prejudiced snob, but I just can't picture this country hick asking an intelligent question about the paintings. Or even about stalactites.

Beats me why, but I don't want to hear him say something embarrassingly inane. It would pain me to watch the others in the group—most of them tourists from big cities—choke down giggles while stealing glances at the thickheaded hayseed.

After all, I've had sex with that hayseed repeatedly in my dreams!

Nina hands me my flashlight and we start the one-hour tour, which continues without any incidents. Cowboy keeps silent. Others ask lots of good questions about the techniques our ancestors used to paint the animals on the walls. In the Mammoth Hall, everybody gapes in awe at the beauty of the creatures on the ceiling.

I realize just how much I love this place, and that I'll miss serving as a tour guide. It won't be part of my new job in the Paris museum, which has dedicated personnel for that.

When we're done, Nina accompanies the group to the exit. I stay behind for a moment, intrigued by a detail on one of the horses in the Dance Hall that I hadn't noticed before. Or, to be more exact, I had noticed it, but hadn't realized its significance.

I pull my phone out and begin to dictate my observations.

When the Grotto grows quiet, Nina returns by my side. "Ready to leave?"

"Not yet," I say. "You go ahead—I'll lock up."

She nods. "See you at the office later this afternoon?"

I glance at my watch, at the painting, and at the five other horses in the cave that I'd like to study more. "This might take a while, so I can't promise I'll be there before closing time."

"OK." She waves goodbye.

I wave back.

Half an hour later, I'm done. It's only five, so I will catch Nina at the office. She'll be the first to hear my new theory. I smile, brimming with enthusiasm and pride as I stride to the gate. Once I've aired it with Nina, I'll have her transcribe my dictated notes while I call Father.

And after that, I'll go home and begin researching and building arguments to support my hypothesis.

Grinning like an idiot, I pull the door toward me. It resists. I push the handle down and pull harder. The door still resists. I stick the key into the keyhole and try to turn it at the same time as I push the handle down. No luck. I jerk it up. No effect whatsoever.

Oh great.

I whip out my phone but, just as I feared, there's no service. Why, why didn't I listen to Nina and switch to her cell phone carrier? She can usually use her phone close to the gate, while I must leave the Grotto and get away from the limestone to get one or two bars.

OK, let's take stock of the situation.

Everyone is gone. The door has malfunctioned. I'll keep trying, but if I don't manage to open it, I'm stuck here until eight-thirty in the morning.

The light coming in through the upper part of the door made of thick, burglarproof glass is growing dimmer by the minute. In an hour or so it will be dark. I can work through the evening, using my flashlight and my phone. But what about the night? There's nothing to lie on or to cover myself with. And even if the temperature in the Grotto is constant, it'll be too cold for my silk shirt and cotton jacket.

I'm so screwed.

"Dr. Muller," someone calls from the recess to my left.

My eyes widen as I spin around.

Cowboy takes a step forward. "Apologies if I spooked you."

I'm still too startled to produce a verbal response.

He gives me a sheepish smile. "I stayed behind, hoping to ask you about that painting over there."

I look in the direction he's pointing.

"Is that a child's hand?" he asks. "Looks like that to me, but since you never commented on it, I wasn't sure."

Oh, so he did look at the art and not just at me!

He even listened to my commentary.

Finally, my tongue recovers its mobility.

"It is a child's hand," I say. "But, much more importantly, do you have a phone?"

5

NATHAN

"Yes," I say. "I do."

"Can I use it?"

I fish my phone out of the pocket of my jeans and hand it to her.

"*Merde!*" She points at the screen.

I raise my eyebrows, surprised to hear her curse.

"*Merde, merde, merde!*" She squeezes her eyes shut, takes a deep breath, and opens them, looking calmer. "No signal."

"Try another spot?"

She shakes her head. "If it doesn't work here, it won't work anywhere else in the cave."

"Would you like me to have a go at the lock?"

Her eyes light up. "Will you? You might be better at this sort of thing than I am."

She hands me the keys.

I begin to tinker with the lock, which shows no intention of giving in. But I've never been a quitter, so I persist.

Clarissa folds her arms over her chest and watches me.

This sort of thing, huh?

She must be referring to all the nonintellectual, *physical* stuff that I do with my hands day in and day out. Does she know what my occupation is? Then again, do I look like the eggheads Celine raves about? Nope. I look like someone who could easily gobble one of them for dinner.

"Damn lock!" I puff, frustrated with my lack of success at the "sort of thing" I'm supposed to be good at.

When I hand the keys back to Clarissa, she narrows her eyes. "Did you have something to do with this?"

I frown. *Whatever does she mean?*

She stares at me and then at the lock.

My frown deepens.

She curls her lip as if to say, *Should I draw you a picture?*

Comprehension hits me. Exasperation and anger come next. "Really? Is that what you think?"

"We never had the slightest problem with this

lock," she says through her clenched jaw. "It's been tampered with. And, yes, I think it was you."

"Hell, no!"

She blinks, taken aback at the vehemence of my reaction.

OK, calm down, Nathan, and put your cards on the table. Given the circumstances, it's the best thing to do.

"The first time I took your tour," I say, "it was to learn about the paintings."

I pause, searching for words.

"And the second?" she prompts.

"The second time was to get a better look at you." I cock my head. "And so were the third, fourth, and fifth times."

She juts her chin up. "So, you admit to interfering with the lock?"

"I admit no such thing. Today's tour was my last attempt to establish eye contact and get a sense of how you'd react to me. When that failed, I lingered so I could walk out at the same time as you and strike up a conversation. That's all, Clarissa. No foul play."

I fold my arms across my chest, mirroring her posture, and wait for her to decide if she believes me. For a long moment, neither of us moves. Clarissa glares at me, and with every passing second, I lose hope.

Now that my righteous anger has dried up, there's no denying that the situation does look fishy from her vantage point. In her place, I'd probably suspect me of trapping her here, too.

Do I come across as a stalker?

Is she *scared* of me?

Jeez, and then I up and call her Clarissa, when I'm not even supposed to know her middle name!

Just as I begin to panic, she sighs and gives me a feeble smile. "Nina told me you've been asking her lots of questions about me."

I nod, still too tense to smile back.

"Nathaniel Girault, right?" She holds her hand out.

"Nathan, please." I shake it, relief washing over me. "Sounds like you've asked her a question or two of your own."

Clarissa's smile widens. "Nina likes you. She was disappointed when she realized what you were after when you chatted with her."

"I didn't mean to—" I begin.

She waves her hand dismissively. "That's OK. Nina's over it. I believe she's been dating someone lately."

"Good for her." I hesitate, before asking, "Am I off the hook, premeditation-wise?"

"Hmm... Considering all the good things Nina and Anne-Chantal have said about you... I guess you are."

"Anne-Chantal?" *Meddling old—Urgh!* "What did she have to say?"

"Not much."

Clarissa's smile grows playful—the most kittenish I've ever seen on her.

God, I love that smile! I want to drink it in.

"She said she's friends with your mom," Clarissa says, "and that you've been her favorite since your most tender age."

I roll my eyes skyward.

She tucks her bottom lip in with her teeth. "Your champion also reported how she changed your diapers when you were a baby, and that you were the cutest and sweetest baby boy she'd ever laid eyes on."

Shoot me now.

"She also said"—Clarissa pauses to gaze at me with an innocence that's so blatantly fake it isn't even trying to pass for authentic—"that you've grown up to be the handsomest young man in the area, and quite possibly in the whole world, that you're single at the moment, that you work really hard running your operation, which is *big* and *profitable*, that—"

"Enough. Please." My face is on fire.

"I'm sorry." She surveys me. "It was unkind of me to tease you like that... even though I wasn't exaggerating. She really did say all of those things."

"I'm sure she did."

"Please don't be angry with her. She meant well."

"Uh-huh."

I'm not angry, but I'm having words with Anne-Chantal next time she shows up at the farm.

Clarissa picks up her flashlight. "Since we're stuck here, anyway, I'm going to head back into the Dance Hall to work for a bit."

"Mind if I tag along?" I point my chin at the flashlight. "I can hold it so your hands are free."

She hesitates a split second and hands me the flashlight. "Sure. Thanks."

We backtrack to one of the inner caves, where she halts in front of a horse painted in black charcoal and ochre, and points to its hooves. "See how the feet are twisted in an unnatural way?"

I bring the flashlight closer to the hooves and study them. "You're right."

"I believe this painting had an educational value. The artist was trying to show, perhaps to children, what tracks this animal would leave."

I tilt my head to the side and inspect the horse's feet again, this time considering Clarissa's hunch.

"It might seem like small fry to you," she says. "But to a young archeologist, that kind of finding could potentially be huge. Career-making huge."

I turn to her. "I don't think it's small fry. As someone who spends most of his days around animals,

I think it's an amazing insight. You should be very proud of yourself."

She beams happily.

One more Clarissa smile I'd never seen before!

As I peer at her lovely face made even lovelier by her toothy grin, time seems to stop. She stares back as her smile fades slowly, and her cheeks begin to redden. I lean forward ever so slightly, my eyes still locked with hers. Clarissa's hand shoots to the side of her neck and strokes it. When my gaze shifts to her mouth, her blush deepens.

Could that mean...?

Does Ice Ice Baby, as Celine sometimes calls her, want me?

Emboldened I take a step forward.

As if waking up from a trance, Clarissa jerks her hand from her neck and balls it into a fist.

I freeze.

She pulls the zipper of her thin jacket all the way up and turns toward the wall. "Do you mind pointing the flashlight at the horse's feet again?"

"Of course."

She turns her phone recorder on and describes every part of the horse and every tiny detail of its twisted feet. When she's done describing, Clarissa begins to develop her theory on the "educational" function of the painting. From there, she talks about the purpose of cave art in general.

When she pauses to collect her thoughts, I toggle the flashlight off. "Saving your batteries."

She says nothing, but it's obvious she's uncomfortable in the dark. So, I pull an app on my phone that lights up my screen instead. The light is dim but it will do.

"Not worried *your* batteries will die?" she asks.

I shake my head. "They'll die on the altar of science."

"Father could've said that." She chuckles. "*Without* the tongue-in-cheek."

"Really?"

"He'd say, 'Penelope, the advancement of science should always be uppermost in your mind.'"

I lower my brows. "You're messing with me. Nobody speaks like that."

"He does."

"What would your mom say?"

"Hmm." She rubs her chin, thinking. "She'd say, 'Penelope, there's no progress without sacrifice.'"

"OK, you *are* messing with me. There's no way both call you Penelope when you prefer Clarissa."

"But *they* prefer Penelope, and that's what they call me."

"They must have a nickname for Penelope." I wrinkle my brow. "Ellie?"

"No."

"Nellie?"

"Uh-uh."

"Pen?"

"They don't use diminutives."

"OK." I hesitate before asking the next question. "Why do you prefer Clarissa to Penelope?"

She sighs. "You mean, it's just as long, right?"

"No—"

"It isn't entirely wrong," she says. "But my closest friends call me Clarissa. They've done so since we were in Cambridge together—"

"You went to Cambridge?"

Of course, she did.

Clarissa nods.

I lean against a stalagmite column and cross my ankles, trying to play it cool. "I went there, too."

Her brows fly up.

"For a visit," I add. "The summer I backpacked around Europe with my buds."

She smiles.

"So, you like the name Clarissa?" I ask.

"I don't like the name as such, but I like being called it."

"What do you mean?"

"When someone calls me Clarissa, it momentarily erases from my mind the litany I grew up with."

"Which is?"

"That I'm a fourth-generation archeologist on both sides, and that I'm destined for 'great things.' "

"Ouch," I say. "Heavy stuff."

"Very heavy. But as Clarissa, I can be a regular girl who sometimes goes to the movies to watch a dumb comedy and who enjoys shopping for clothes."

"In short, who has fun."

She nods.

"Are you an only child?" I ask.

"Yes. I wish I had a sibling, so he or she could carry half of my burden."

"Amen," I say. "I could sign under that."

"Only child, too?"

"Yeah..."

"The future of the farm? The savior? Last hope of the rural world?" She gives me a wink. "Daddy's hero?"

"Yes, to the first three, but not to the last one. It's Pop who was my hero."

"Not anymore?"

I run my hand through my hair. "He passed ten years ago."

"I'm sorry." She hugs herself and rubs her arms.

"You're cold."

"A little."

"Here, put this on." I take off my padded leather jacket and hand it to her.

She shakes her head. "Are you crazy? You'll freeze."

"It would take more than this for me to freeze," I say, laughing. "Besides, my sweater is a lot warmer than what you have under your flimsy jacket."

"How about we swap?"

I tilt my head to one side and just stare at her, letting her realize the ridiculousness of her proposition.

"Right." Her gaze shifts from my face to my chest. "You could throw my jacket over your right shoulder."

I snort.

"Or the left one," she adds, a smile crinkling her eyes, "if it's more sensitive to the cold."

"How about a compromise?"

"Listening."

"You put my jacket over your jacket, and we transfer to the nook where I was waiting for you," I say. "It has a bench to sit on and it's closer to the door, in case someone notices one of us is missing and comes looking."

"Deal! My mind is too foggy now to continue working, anyway."

Murmuring a thank-you, Clarissa turns toward the wall. I help her into my jacket, which hangs down to her mid thigh, and with sleeves so long her hands get lost.

She turns back toward me, smiling, closes her eyes and takes a deep breath, flaring her nostrils.

Uh-oh.

Seized by panic, I scrutinize her for signs of disgust. What if my jacket reeks of manure or—worse—sweat, both of which I've grown desensitized to over the years? I make a point of keeping my body and clothes clean, but people have different thresholds for smells.

"Holy cow!" She opens her eyes.

My panic level is about to go through the rock above our heads.

Clarissa grins. "Feels like I've been dropped into a sea of testosterone."

Is that a bad thing? Or good?

"It's surprisingly homey," she says, answering my unspoken question.

Homey.

I let out the breath I was holding. Even if "homey" is a Parisian euphemism for "smelly," in situations like this, the best thing to do is stick to the facts.

Fact number one: She didn't return my jacket.

Fact number two: Right now, she's pulling its collar up as if to take in more "homeyness."

All is not lost.

I point my phone's light at the ground so we can see where we step and offer her my hand.

After a brief hesitation, she pushes the sleeve of the jacket up to free her beautiful hand and places it into my open palm. Her touch is soft—and electrifying. I close my fingers over her hand, and start walking slowly. We reach the nook much too soon.

With difficulty, I let go of her hand.

Clarissa scoots to the right side of the bench and pats the space next to her. "Plenty of room for both."

Nodding, I sit down and place the phone between us.

An awkward silence follows, during which I try hard not to think about the sleeping arrangements we'll need to discuss soon.

Except, that's all I can think about.

Even the smartphone next to me—the ultimate twenty-first-century gadget—makes me think of a medieval "sword of honor" trick I'd read about somewhere. A knight would place it between himself and a lady who wasn't his wife if circumstances forced them to sleep next to each other.

Thing is, Clarissa may well be a lady who isn't my wife, but I'm no knight in shining armor.

I fully intend to use our circumstances to my advantage.

6

NATHAN

"It's eight," Clarissa says, looking at her wristwatch. "The best thing to do now would be to sleep, but it's too early, and... um... I don't think I can sleep sitting, or lying on the cold floor, for that matter."

Aha! I wasn't the only one thinking about our sleeping arrangements.

It's very tempting to suggest that my body would make for an excellent mattress, but I hold my tongue. While she obviously has a sense of humor, she's still a refined city girl, unaccustomed to the plainspoken ways of the country.

Tread carefully, Nathan.

"You can try to sleep on the bench," I say.

"What about you?" She clears her throat. "That's the only bench inside the Grotto."

"I'll be fine on the floor."

A deep crease forms between her brows.

Not good. She's fretting.

Time to change the topic. "Just before you stopped recording, you said something about how that horse's twisted feet could change our idea of cave art."

"Yes, well, I was getting ahead of myself." She tucks her hair behind her ears. "I'll need a lot more evidence and research before I can make that claim in public."

"Humor me—I'm not here to judge you."

She gives me a sidelong look. "This stays between us, OK? I may be completely off the mark here."

"Mum's the word." I draw an invisible zipper over my mouth. "If I *really* need to talk about it, I'll unburden myself to my herd's head cow. She's second to none at keeping secrets."

Clarissa gives me a nod. "OK. So, you see, archeologists are still not sure why cave dwellers made art. One big theory is that they would get bored, sitting around after a meal, not doing anything special. So some of them made up tales. Others made graffiti."

"It figures. I sing when I'm bored."

"Will you sing for me?"

"Maybe later." I flash her a smile. "But, please, go on. Is there another theory?"

"The other big theory is that making those paintings was part of some ritual."

"What kind of ritual?"

"Nobody knows."

"Hmm..." I scratch the back of my head. "I don't like that theory."

She raises her eyebrows. "Why not?"

"It's too easy." I shrug before saying, in what I hope is a professorial voice, "When clueless about why folks did what they did, call it a ritual."

She turns toward me—not just her head, but her entire body—and leans forward. "That's exactly how I feel about it."

"So what's *your* theory?"

She stares into my eyes for a moment, before speaking. "The horse in the Dance Room would suggest that at least some of the paintings were made with the purpose of recording and transmitting practical knowledge. They had an educational function."

"Makes sense to me."

She beams. "Really?"

"I'd wager that paint was a lot harder to produce in those days than now, so if I were a caveman, I'd make sure my art did double duty."

She blinks and stares at me like I've just given her a

map to the Holy Grail. "That's an excellent point, Nathan!"

"Happy to help, ma'am."

"Naturally, I'll need to find many other examples in other caves before I can postulate a theory," she says.

I give her a solemn nod. "Naturally."

"I wouldn't want to make a fool of myself." There's that crease again.

"Mum's the word, trust me."

She nods. "I trust you."

We stare into each other's eyes for a long moment. Clarissa's gaze is filled with excitement, and something else, something a pessimist would describe as warmth, and an optimist, as longing.

I'm an optimist.

My body tenses, aching for her touch. My hand on the bench burns to inch closer to hers and brush it. But my instincts tell me it's too soon. Clarissa is just beginning to see a man with a functioning brain behind the jacked hick.

She isn't flirting with me yet.

Hold your horses, Nathan.

"Speaking of horses," I say before correcting myself, "I mean, education, do you think that was also the purpose of *that* shape?"

I stride to the opposite wall and point the beam of the flashlight up at what looks like an erect penis.

She comes near me and says without batting an eye, "The phallus?"

What a handy word! "Yes, the phallus. Do you believe it was a teaching aid for a lesson in human anatomy?"

She smiles. "That's a bit far-fetched but can't be excluded."

"Do you think it's life-size?"

"I don't think so." She tilts her head to the side and squints. "It's much too large."

Er... not really.

"There are men," I say, "Living men, who would compare favorably."

My traitorous eyes dart to my fly before I look up at the wall again.

Clarissa is silent.

No giggling, no comment, not a sound.

Shit. I went too far.

Discussing cave-art phalluses is one thing, but drawing her attention to my real cock is quite another.

She's going to bristle. She won't want to speak to me anymore.

"Those men, they sound... *intimidating*," Clarissa finally says, laughter in her voice.

My whole body slackens in relief. "They aren't! Their... phalluses aren't *freakishly* big."

"Then, how would you describe them?"

An adjective, quick! One that would both reassure and entice her, one that won't be too vulgar or too—

Her lips twitch. "Would you call them *fulfilling*?"

Yes! "That's exactly what I would call them."

My eyes drill into hers.

She holds my gaze and begins to stroke the back of her neck as she did earlier in front of the horse with twisted hooves.

Dude—she's flirting.

In fact, she's beyond flirting.

Consciously or not, Clarissa is *seducing* me.

My eyes wander over her face and body. Suddenly, brushing her hand is not enough. It won't even scratch the surface of my wanting.

Need to hold her, all of her, need to press her to me.

My control snapping, I place the flashlight on the ground, lunge forward, and grip her shoulders. The next second, my lips descend on hers, kissing and coaxing her to open up. I pull her closer to my chest, almost crushing her soft breasts. My hands roam freely, exploring the shape of her.

So fucking good.

Clarissa doesn't resist me, doesn't push me away. Better still, her eyes become hooded as she melts into me. She wants me, there's no doubt about it, but... she's too passive. Her arms hang at her sides. She's turned her face up toward me, but she hasn't parted her lips.

Is this her way?

Nah. It doesn't track.

Driven, independent women like her don't make inert lovers. Something's holding her back.

"Rissa," I whisper against her mouth. "It's OK. Let go—I have you."

I have no idea why I called her Rissa. Nor do I fully understand what I've asked her to let go of. But, somehow, it feels right. Both felt right.

On a gasp, she parts her lips.

I push my tongue between them and devour her sweet mouth. Can't get enough of her taste. Standing on tiptoe, she kisses me with passion. As our tongues dance together, she lifts her arms and grips my neck.

I back her against the closest stalagmite column, and allow my erection to prod her tummy through her layers of clothing.

Will she shrink from it?

Rissa moans softly and pushes into me. Sweet Jesus, she's pressing her taut stomach against my cock. I begin to grind, all while kissing her and fondling her breasts.

And then her right hand lets go of my neck and settles, fingers splayed, on my bulge.

Inert, you say?

Bending my knees, I reach for the hem of her narrow skirt and push it up her smooth thighs. Up, up, up, until the skirt is bunched around her waist. Then I make quick work of unzipping both jackets.

Need to see her.

Tearing my mouth from hers, I draw back a notch and look at her. "Oh my God, Rissa..."

The sight before me is sexier than anything I've seen.

My cock twitches beneath her palm. She smiles.

She's killing me.

Her legs, clad in tight little boots and stay-up stockings, are long and shapely. Made to be stroked and kissed. She's wearing black panties with a bit of lace. I picture them dangling from one of her ankles, her legs wrapped around my waist, ankles crossed, squeezing me as I fill her.

Whoa, going too fast, Nathan!

I shoo that image away... only to make room for another one in which her legs are on my shoulders.

That's it, I must touch her. I simply can't go on living if I don't.

I cup her between her legs and find she's already wet.

"Yes, please," she whispers, nuzzling the side of my face.

I must have died and gone to heaven.

She throbs under my fingers, pressing into them. When I push the crotch of her panties aside and slip in a finger, she lets out a ragged moan and clenches her muscles around it. I'm loving how wet and eager Rissa is. What I'm loving a lot less is that she's tight.

Much too tight.

Truth is, calling my cock "fulfilling" rather than "freakish" doesn't shrink it to... manageable proportions. I'm not complaining. Better too large than too small, right? But experience tells me she might recoil when she sees it.

With her hand still on my cock, she gives it a gentle upward stroke. "You weren't lying about your size."

My lids grow heavy. "Why would I?"

"Men often do."

She trails her hand down, then up again. Her fingers reach the buckle of my belt and stop there.

Will she undo it? Will she free my cock and stroke it, skin to skin? What will her expression be when she looks at it?

My hand is still between her legs, but I've stopped thrusting.

She takes my wrist and pulls my hand away from her. "We'll continue this later."

"Promise?"

"Oh, yes."

I wait for her next move.

Slowly, she unbuckles my belt and opens the fly of

my jeans. Her gaze locks with mine as she fumbles with my underwear, freeing my raging erection.

Her fingers begin to explore me, but she won't look down.

Is she panicked by what she'll see? I try to read her expression, but I'm too crazed with lust to play shrink.

"Look at it, Rissa," I say softly.

She gives me a tight little smile and lowers her eyes. "Oh my."

Hooking my index finger under her chin, I tip her head up to see her face. Rissa's eyes are wide, but there's no distress or, worse, dread in them.

That's a start.

"You were telling the truth," she says. "The one on the wall can't hold a candle to it."

I arch an eyebrow in mock affront. "I'd never lie about something so sacred."

She giggles.

So far so good.

"It's too big for me," she says just as I begin to relax.

"You don't know that."

She looks down and studies me. "It's absolutely gorgeous, Nathan, but if you... it'll hurt me if you—"

"Shush." I press a finger against her lips. "Hurting you is the last thing I want."

"I know."

I brush a gentle kiss on her mouth. "You don't have

to decide anything now. We can just fool around and see where it leads us."

"OK." She gives me a relieved smile and tightens her grip on my cock. "I've never seen anything like this. It's a privilege."

"Is it?"

She nods. "May I?"

Before I realize what she's asking, she squats and gives the tip of my cock a tentative lick. I shudder, my hips twitching involuntarily. She licks again and again, stroking the base with her hands, squeezing gently and kissing it.

When she looks up at me, her gaze is dark and intense.

"I'll come if you don't stop now," I rasp.

"That's OK."

"No." I grab her shoulders and pull her up. "Ladies first."

"You fiend," she protests. "I was enjoying myself!"

"I have principles."

"They are too old-fashioned."

I shrug.

"So what do you suggest?"

"For starters,"—I hook my thumbs into her lacy panties at the sides and pull them down—"we get rid of these."

She helps me remove her panties. I leave the rest of

her clothing on, so she won't be too cold. Her pubes are dark and only lightly trimmed, which is a godsend for a man who's never liked bald pussy. Reaching down, I play with her moist curls and spread her folds, exposing her hooded little bud. My breath hitches and my cock pulses like crazy as I stare at her.

She lets out an amused snort. "You look like you could eat me."

"That's the plan."

She chuckles.

"Lean back on the column," I say, my voice coarse.

She does immediately.

I kneel before her and settle her right thigh on my shoulder.

And then I carry out my plan.

7

CLARISSA

Nathan tongues me like I'm the world's most delicious ice cream.

His fingers stretch and probe.

I tangle my fingers in his hair as I moan.

He abrades my sensitive skin with his evening stubble, and I love it.

When my legs begin to tremble, he wraps his big hands around my bottom and squeezes, his mouth still doing its magic between my legs.

In a rush of heat and exquisite pleasure, I shudder. Then another wave, and one more. Barely conscious of my surroundings, I hear myself making strange noises, mumbling between groans and whimpers. "Oh God... Nathan... I can't... Oh God." It's too much. I want him to stop.

I don't want him to stop.

As I ride the last aftershock, he strokes my hips and trails his tongue up to my stomach. He rises and leans his forehead against mine.

I encase his face between my hands and kiss him deeply.

A long moment later, we break the kiss. Nathan stares at my face and then at my bared sex, his gaze scalding me.

"Still hungry?" I tease.

He doesn't respond, doesn't even smile back.

Heat creeps up my neck and cheeks.

Who knew being selectively undressed like this would make me feel more bared—and more turned on —than full nudity?

My heart quickening, I lower my gaze to his enormous shaft. I want it as much as I'm apprehensive about it. What will I do when he presses its tip against my entrance? How will my body react? Can I stretch enough to receive it without pain?

But he said I didn't have to decide yet.

He said we could just fool around.

Gingerly, I palm him and begin to stroke up and down his hot length. He groans, one hand on the column next to my head, the other on the side of my neck. I rub a little harder, curling my fingers around him. He throbs against my palm.

I look up into his heavy-lidded eyes. "May I?"

A nod.

Finally.

I've been burning to press my lips around it since I first saw it. As I explore its hard shape, its cordlike veins and the softness of its skin against my lips and tongue, I feel like an ancient priestess performing an act of worship.

If that phallus on the wall is life-size, then the man it was attached to must have had quite a following. I envy his groupies who were no doubt sturdier than I am and more apt to accommodate him.

Were all the women Nathan slept with able to take him in? Would he tell me the truth if I ask him? It's damn tempting to ask.

Except, I won't.

Asking him about his exes might give him the wrong idea. Regardless of how he makes me feel or what happens here tonight, I'm not going to date a farmer from Verlezy. We belong in different worlds, and the only bridge between those worlds is our lust.

Lust fades away. Complications remain.

OK, if tonight is all we have, I'd better shut that chatterbox in my head and let my hair down.

I increase my pace and the amount of pressure, feeling him grow even harder, thicker and bigger than he already is. Wetness pools again between my legs. My core is heavy, empty, wanting to be filled.

"Rissa," he murmurs. "Careful, or I'll come."

I lift my eyes to him.

He smooths his hand on my cheek, his eyes drilling into mine, searching.

With my hands tight on his shaft, I pull back a little and bite my lower lip. "That's the plan."

"Really?" He searches my face.

Slowly, I nod.

He trails the pad of his thumb over my mouth. "You know, you've let me do that already in my fantasies. Many times. But I had no idea you'd be up for it in real life."

"Appearances can be deceiving," I say, omitting to mention I've never actually tried it before.

The mere thought of such an act had appeared distasteful.

Except, with Nathan, it doesn't.

He grips the nape of my head and guides me gently back to his groin. A few enthusiastic minutes later, his face contorts in pleasure and pain. I find that both beautiful and empowering.

He growls, pumping, visibly struggling to hold his peak off a little longer.

And then his warm seed fills my mouth.

When he's done, I wipe my lips and laugh nervously, feeling a little awkward.

"It was fun," I say, standing up.

I pull the hem of my skirt down, ignoring the aching and clenching in my center.

One can't have everything. He's too big for me.

But even without penetration, I just had the sexiest time in my life, and that will have to do.

Nathan picks up the now-flickering flashlight and offers me his hand. Back at the bench, we sit down next to each other, our knees touching.

He turns to me. "Will you come sit on my lap?"

"I thought you'd never ask!"

The frankness of my reply startles me.

Nathan looks a little surprised, too.

And happy.

The moment my butt touches his thighs, he puts his arms around me and pulls me closer. "Rissa."

That moniker, said in a deep, gravelly voice feels like a caress. Loving. Tender. Doing unwanted things to my heart.

Watch out, Clarissa.

I trace his firm jawline. "I have a nickname for you, too, you know."

"Tell me."

"Cowboy."

He laughs. "Did you just come up with it?"

"No, that's what I've been calling you since your fourth visit when Nina told me what you did for a living."

"I'm afraid what I do is a lot less romantic than what you see in movies," he says, before cocking his head. "So, you spotted me a while ago."

I nod, caught red-handed.

He gives me a long look, and I know what he's thinking even if the question never comes.

I give him an apologetic smile. "I didn't want to give you a chance to ask me out."

Wow. That came out a lot more brutal than I intended.

"I figured that much," he says.

"Why didn't you ever ask me a question during the tour?" I smooth the back of my hand against his cheek, enjoying the prickliness of his stubble. "Everyone else did, but you never said a word. You just stared."

He shrugs. "I had lots of questions, but I thought they were dumb. I didn't want to ruin my already slim chances with you."

"The questions you asked tonight, and the observations you made were anything but dumb," I say. "Even my parents would concede that much."

"I take it they have lofty standards?"

I roll my eyes. "You have no idea. I'm a fourth-generation archeologist on both sides, so they expect me to be the next Champollion."

"The name sounds familiar... Who's that?"

"The guy who cracked Egyptian hieroglyphs in the nineteenth century."

He nods. "That's a tall order."

I skew a smile. "Not for Penelope Clarissa Muller. They seriously expect the Nobel Committee will one day have to add a new prize category in archeology just to celebrate my achievements."

"You're lucky," he says.

I draw my eyebrows together. "Is that a joke?"

"Nope." He kisses my hand as I trail it across his mouth. "You have parents who believe you're super smart and can do anything."

"Do you realize the pressure that puts on me? I feel that no matter how hard I work, I'm bound to disappoint them."

"Right," he says. "I hadn't considered that part."

I peer at him. "What about your parents? I bet your mom thinks you're a national treasure, and your dad must have been very proud of you."

"It's hard to know what Ma thinks of me," he says with a smirk. "Except that it's my sacred duty to make sure it's handed down to the next generation."

I frown.

"Don't get me wrong," he adds quickly. "Ma has a great personality and she loves me. It's just... well, let's just say she may not be convinced I'm the brightest pea in the pod."

My jaw falls. "Why would you say that?"

"Maybe because she and Pop took me out of regular school at sixteen and sent me to an agricultural *lycée*."

"It wasn't what you wanted?"

"I didn't really have time to stop and consider what I wanted. Dad had been so sick, and then I had to deal with the funeral and all the paperwork because Ma was too devastated. She could barely make herself get up in the morning... And then we were hit by the milk crisis."

"I remember seeing angry farmers on TV," I say. "They blocked roads and dumped manure in front of administrative buildings."

"Yeah, well, you'd be angry, too, if you had to pay 45 percent in taxes when the milk price was pushed down to two hundred euros per ton."

"I believe I would." I kiss his nose. "Do you think you would've gone to college, if circumstances had been different?"

He slips a hand under the double layer of our jackets and cups one of my breasts over the blouse. My lids drop with the joy of his warm, big hand on my petite breast.

"Honestly," he says. "I'm not sure I would've gone to college. I did OK at school, but I was never an A student."

I caress his strong neck. "Few boys are at that age. They just take longer to grow up than girls."

"Anyway," he says. "It wasn't in the cards. The year Pop died, his friend and our neighbor—my bestie Celine's dad—took his life. Several farms went belly up... But for Ma, selling our farm was out of the question. It was Pop's legacy. He'd sacrificed himself for it."

"What do you mean?"

"He died of cancer caused by pesticide exposure. You see, he'd been in charge of spraying since he was ten, and he'd never used a mask or gloves."

"How awful!"

He nods.

"You loved him very much, didn't you?" I ask.

"I worshiped him."

We stroke each other in silence for a while.

I wonder if Nathan will ask me if he can see me again. For his sake, I hope he doesn't. He won't like my reply.

"Do you have a boyfriend in Paris?" he asks.

I shake my head, dreading the next question.

But when it comes, it isn't what I expected. "How long has it been since you had sex?"

"A long time." I hesitate. "Eighteen months."

He sucks in a breath, but says nothing.

The flashlight battery dies a few minutes later.

When Nathan moves to turn his phone on, I grab his hand to stop him. "We should try to get some sleep."

"Yes, we should." He picks me up and lowers me onto the bench. "Put your head on my lap, and lie down."

"What about you?"

"I can sleep sitting," he says. "I've done it before."

I stretch out on the bench and fall asleep within minutes with my face to his groin and his hand in my hair.

ANNE-CHANTAL'S LAUGHING voice wakes us up in the morning. "What a picture!"

I sit up and look at my watch. It's seven in the morning.

Thank God, she showed up to work an hour early!

When I glance at Nathan before I return his jacket, he's peering at her, eyes narrowed and eyebrows lowered. That prompts me to pay closer attention.

The cashier doesn't look shocked to discover us here.

She doesn't even look surprised.

In fact, she looks mighty pleased with herself.

8

NATHAN

Ma is back from her vacation, cooking a homecoming dinner.

Celine, Frau Lotte, and Lorenzo are also in the kitchen, supposedly giving Ma a hand, but are really just sipping wine and talking about organic fertilizers. That is, Celine is doing most of the talking and the others are doing most of the sipping.

I can hear everyone's voices very distinctly from the computer room where I'm toiling with an endless EU questionnaire. Ma never touches them, but one day she's going to have to sit down and learn. I hate paperwork as much as she does, so it's only fair that we take turns.

After Anne-Chantal freed us yesterday morning, Rissa said she needed to go home for a few hours. She had her own car and didn't need me to give her a lift. Once she left, I tried to pressure Ma's chum to confess to jamming the lock.

She folded her arms across her generous bosom. "Someone had to do something. It was becoming unbearable to watch you waste away like that."

"So, you confess—"

"I confess to nothing at all." She lifted her chin to the locksmith working on the door. "He'll confirm it was a malfunction."

I rolled my eyes, not bothering to ask Marcel, our village locksmith and Anne-Chantal's dear husband, for confirmation.

Before I left the Grotto, I discreetly placed my phone under the bench, next to an eyeglasses case that must have fallen out of Rissa's handbag. With a bit of luck, she'd be the one to find it when she came looking for her glasses. That would give her a pretext to get in touch.

Still under the spell of our intimacy in the cave, I was hopeful, almost certain she'd show up last night. Or at least reach out via Anne-Chantal, inviting me to come by and collect my phone.

But she didn't.

Not last night, nor this morning before work. And now, with a rainstorm howling outside, bending trees and threatening to blow roofs away, there's no way she'll turn up.

The doorbell rings.

I open the door, expecting Lorenzo's girlfriend Paola, who always arrives at least twenty minutes late.

Except it isn't Paola—it's Rissa.

"Your phone," she says, handing me the device.

"Thank you."

We stare at each other.

"I better go," she begins.

"Stay." I clear my throat. "Ma is cooking boeuf bourguignon tonight, her specialty. We have a few people over for dinner."

She hesitates. "I don't want to intrude."

"Don't be daft." I point to the uproar outside. "It'll be safer to drive back in a couple of hours when the storm quiets down."

She glances at the sky, at her car, and then back at me. "OK. Thank you."

When we enter the kitchen, four pairs of eyes zero in on her and shift to me.

"Hi everyone," she says, giving them a timid little smile.

Well done, Rissa!

If I were in her place now, with Celine, Lorenzo and—especially—Ma eyeballing me like that, I think I'd just go into a stupor.

They all greet her.

"This is Clarissa," I say. "I invited her to join us for dinner."

Celine jumps up and puts an extra plate, glass and silverware on the table.

Respect, she mouths to me when Rissa isn't looking.

Lorenzo fills her glass. Ma stirs the brew on the stove with her back to us. I wonder what she's thinking.

The doorbell rings again, and this time it's Paola.

Ma announces that the food is ready and can everyone please sit down.

I serve.

"If I knew we had a special guest tonight, I would've laid the table in the dining room," Ma says, taking her serving of fragrant bourguignon from me.

Celine pats her hand. "Your kitchen is just as presentable, Brigitte."

"I know," Ma says. "But still."

Paola turns to Rissa. "Are you a local farmer, too?"

Celine snorts.

"I'm an archeologist," Rissa says with a smile. "I curate the museum at the Darcy Grotto near Auxerre."

Lorenzo perks up. "We were planning to go there next weekend!"

The conversation flows smoothly, mostly between

the volunteers, Celine, and Rissa. I keep silent, listening and staring at Rissa.

So does Ma.

When Lorenzo, Frau Lotte and I finish our second servings, Ma ushers everyone to the TV room for tea and cookies.

Rissa giggles over something Celine whispers in her ear. I swallow my cookie and scoot closer on the couch to where Rissa is sitting.

"What about the public library in Auxerre?" she asks Celine.

My friend sighs. "All female stuff."

"Have you tried your luck in Dijon?" Rissa asks. "It has several libraries."

Oh, I see. Celine has told her about her hot nerd fetish.

"I have," she says. "And I even spotted there two adorable guys who were totally my type and weren't wearing wedding rings."

"And?" Rissa leans forward, bright-eyed.

Celine shrugs. "And, crickets. Both made it clear they weren't interested."

"Um... Have you considered tweaking your look a little bit?" Rissa asks her.

"Why would I do that?"

"It's the combination of cropped hair, lumberjack

shirt, roomy jeans, Doc Martens, and posture." Rissa smiles softly. "It might be giving the men who don't know you the wrong idea."

"Which is?"

"That you're into women."

Frau Lotte, who seems to have overheard Rissa's last remark, turns to Celine, disappointment and shock in her eyes. "You're not?"

Celine blinks, flabbergasted.

Frau Lotte mutters something that sounds like a curse under her breath.

"Jeez, I had no idea." Celine looks at Rissa and at Frau Lotte. "Really?"

Both women nod.

"But I love my lumberjack shirts!" Celine says. "They're part of who I am. And you can't expect me to wear heels on a farm!"

"Of course not," Rissa says.

Celine puffs, stands, and carries her plate to the kitchen. When she reappears in the TV room, her expression is determined.

"Thank you, Brigitte, for the delicious dinner," she says to Ma. "So happy we met, Clarissa! Night, everyone. I'm turning in early so I can process this... revelation."

"I'll be happy to paint your nails and teach you how to use makeup," Paola offers.

Celine nods a thank-you and marches out the door.

One after another, the volunteers retreat to their sleeping quarters. Ma yawns, declares she's too knackered to stay up and heads to her bedroom upstairs.

Rissa and I are the last ones left in the room.

My heart pounds in my chest.

If she didn't mean to spend the night with me, she would've left by now. *Right?*

I stare at her lips.

She stares at mine.

Suddenly, she stands. "Thank you, Nathan. I had a wonderful evening."

"Want to have a look at my cottage before you drive off?" I blurt.

"You don't live in the farmhouse?"

I shake my head and stand. "Follow me."

The moment we enter the cottage and I pull the door closed, I'm kissing her. She kisses me back, opening her mouth to let me in. I thrust in my tongue deep and hard, while my hands tug at her coat.

She lets me remove it.

I'm so impatient my hands are shaking as I throw it over a chair. Her hands are just as unsteady when she pulls on the sides of my jacket.

I shrug it off.

We kiss and kiss, starved for each other, drinking

each other in. My mouth latches to her soft lips with an almost bruising ferocity and a need I'm unable to control. This woman was made for me. I know it in my bones.

Just like I know she'll let me take her tonight.

That's why she's here.

She's going to give it her best shot despite her misgivings and fears that she's too small for me.

I let go of her mouth.

She gasps, eyes glazed with lust.

"I'll be gentle," I whisper near her ear. "I won't give you more than you can take."

She nods once, her nod a profession of trust.

As my hand grips her waist and pulls her to me, my other hand unzips her silky black pants. They fall to the floor and she steps out of them. Slipping a hand inside her panties, I press two fingers to her cleft and rub. She moans. When I plunge them inside her, her moans turn into whimpers.

I kiss her again, pushing my tongue deep, fucking her mouth with it. She grows unsteady on her feet, leaning against me for support. A few more thrusts of my tongue and fingers and she collapses against me.

"Aah," she groans raggedly into my mouth.

My cock is so hard it threatens to make a hole through my jeans or burst them at the seams.

That's it, I'm taking her within the next five minutes or I'll explode.

I pick her up and carry her to the bedroom. We yank on each other's clothes and underwear until we're naked. I open a condom. She helps me roll it on.

I nudge her to lie on her back and rake my gaze over her. "So beautiful. I'm going to kiss you absolutely everywhere, but right now I need to be inside you."

"I need you inside me."

Her face is flushed with an almost desperate longing, and she's dripping wet from my earlier caresses.

It's now or never, Nathan.

Positioning my tip at her entrance, I rub it against her wet curls and push in just a notch. Slowly, her opening begins to stretch, adjusting to me.

She lifts her head, propping herself on her elbows. "I want to watch you enter me."

Another small thrust, then another. More stretching. My gaze travels between her pussy and her face looking out for signs of discomfort. But there are none. Encouraged by that, I thrust again, this time harder.

A throaty gasp escapes Rissa's lips and she arches her back.

Still no sign of pain.

With another push, I'm sheathed deep inside her.

I withdraw slowly and thrust again, careful not to hit her womb. "How's this?"

"It's wonderful," she says. "Absolutely fucking wonderful."

Dropping her head back to the pillow, she grips my neck and wraps her legs around my waist.

As I pump in and out, pleasure builds, held back only by my promise not to give her more than she can take.

"Faster," she commands.

I increase the cadence, and soon we're moving against each other fast and hard like a well-oiled machine. Given how happy she looks and sounds, I'm tempted to push harder still, but I rein in that urge.

As things stand, I don't know if I'll see her again. But if I hurt her, even inadvertently, I can be sure as hell that I won't.

Closing my eyes, I thrust, faster and faster. She writhes beneath me, completely open, throbbing around me, trusting me to give her what she craves.

A few more thrusts, and her pussy begins to spasm. I burn again to push a little deeper while she's riding her orgasm, but I deny myself. This have to do. This is already so much more than I could hope for.

Crying out my name, Rissa shudders. A tremor

shakes her legs and her body, while her mouth opens, forming a beautiful *o*.

The sight of her abandon sends me over the edge.

With each spurt of my seed, the pressure subsides, making room for joy, and a flying sensation that lifts my hard body as if it were a feather.

Afterward, we cuddle in the soft glow of the night-light.

"Turns out I'm roomier than I thought," she says with that deliciously sly smile of hers.

"Told ya."

"Was it good for you? If it was at least half as good as it was for me, I can die happy and proud." She gives me a wink.

I frown in mock concern. "Please don't die just yet. Now that I got a taste, I need more."

She smiles, but gives no promises. Then she looks away.

Not good.

"Did you ever envision selling the farm and the land?" she asks, turning back to me.

"It isn't mine to sell—well, half of it at least. It's Ma's."

"Of course," she says. "And, from what you told me, she'll hold on to it until her last breath."

I nod.

Something infinitely sad flashes in her eyes before she turns away again.

I bring her hand to my mouth and kiss the inside of her wrist. "Farming may not be the most profitable occupation these days, but the land here in Burgundy —and we own a good chunk of it—increases in value every year. That said, Ma's attachment to this land and to this farm is purely sentimental. It was Pop's whole life."

"Is it your whole life, too?"

"Good question." I scratch my head. "I don't know any other life to compare it to."

"So, you have no idea if you'd enjoy doing something else more than operating a dairy farm?"

"I don't think I would."

We lie in silence for a long moment. This conversation isn't about farming, of course. It's about us. It's about the possibility of us being together.

"Do you think you could enjoy living on a farm?" I ask.

She laughs. "I'd be the most ridiculous farmer in the world!"

"I said *live* on a farm, not operate one."

She shakes her head. "In fact, I'm going back to Paris in two weeks, to be part of an extensive research team in one of the capital's best museums."

"What?" I turn on my side and peer at her. "Why? You've only been here a few months!"

"Almost two years, actually," she says. "You only *discovered* me a few months ago."

What do I say to that? That I'd do anything to turn back the time and *discover* her earlier, much earlier? That I'd give a hand to have Anne-Chantal stop by and give me a ticket to a guided tour of the Grotto on Rissa's very first day as its curator? It would be the truth. But there's no point saying it now.

We hug each other.

As I drift away, my body light from the lovemaking and my heart filled to the brim, a heavy, dreamless slumber swallows me up.

Rissa wakes up at dawn and sneaks out while I pretend to be asleep.

The moment she's out the door, I begin to ache for her.

I tell myself it's just my body. My cock, my hands, every limb, and muscle on me.

But not my heart.

It can't be my heart.

Because it takes more than two nights to fall in love.

I must've read that in one of Ma's psychology magazines when I was bored and out of other reading material.

The irony of the situation is that I know Rissa wants me as much as I want her.

But Dr. Penelope Muller wants something else.

And, unfortunately for me, she wins.

9

NATHAN

The traditional Farewell to Winter Ball is in full swing.

OK, the ball isn't a *real* tradition because it hadn't existed until twenty years ago. Then one year, Josephine, the wife of our eternally reelected mayor, introduced the extravaganza and got the d'Arcy family to sponsor it.

I guess that's the reason Count Sebastian d'Arcy is always in attendance.

And the reason the good citizens of Verlezy and the neighboring villages gather in the town hall, suffer through a speech or two, and then eat, drink, and dance into the wee hours of the morning.

Celine and Ma always drag me to the ball.

They don't do it for my sake, mind you. I'm just the

inextricable owner of the two male arms they like to lean on when entering the town hall.

This year is no different.

No, it *is* different. While I'd normally look forward to chugging down some beers with my buds and maybe sneaking off with a local woman, tonight I'm not in the right mood for either.

I haven't been in the right mood for twelve days now, ever since Rissa spent a night at my cottage and announced she was going back to Paris.

"Oh, come on!" Celine nudges me with her elbow. "Stop sulking."

I force a smile.

"Do you notice something different about me?" she asks.

I study her face. "You're wearing lipstick."

"What else?"

"Um... mascara?"

"Yes!" She beams. "Anything else?"

"If this is a quiz, do I get a beer for three correct answers?"

She rolls her eyes and huffs.

"She's wearing a skirt," Ma says. "A skirt!"

I look down to verify that improbable claim. It's safe to say I've seen Celine almost every single day of her life—she's two years my junior—and never, not once, has she worn a skirt.

But today she is.

"It's not too awful," she says. "As long as I remember to keep my knees together when I sit. But the heels, they're killing me."

As if to confirm her statement, she trips and spills some of her beer on the floor.

Ma pats her cheek.

My friends Danny and Mo wave from the middle of the room and saunter over. As Celine and I chat with them, I can't help wondering if Rissa will make an appearance alone or in the company of her colleagues.

"Hey, Nathan!" someone calls from the entrance.

A moment later, Thomas, my second cousin on Pop's side, joins our group. "Good evening, Brigitte."

"Haven't seen you in… forever." Ma gives him a hug. "What are you doing here?"

"Just passing," he says noncommittally.

Thomas studied advanced mathematics but instead of applying for academic jobs when he graduated, he chose to use his math skills in banking. Turned out to be a great move. For the last six or seven years, he's been working for an investment bank in Dijon, developing financial models, and amassing millions.

"So, what do you do for a living?" Danny asks Thomas.

He pushes his eyeglasses up the bridge of his nose. "I'm a mathematician."

"Hot nerd alert," Celine whispers to me.

I take another look at Thomas, and it hits me how much he fits her type.

She should totally go for it.

But the poor thing is too awestruck to utter a word. She downs her second glass and mumbles, "Need another one."

Poor Celine.

Ma and I exchange a look as Celine scurries away.

When Danny and Mo move on, Ma arches an eyebrow at Thomas. "So, what did you say you were doing here?"

"I'm looking for a house to buy."

"Moving to the country?" Ma asks.

He smiles. "No, just as a getaway. And a quiet retreat for when I want to do some hardcore math."

Celine slips and falls in the center of the room, causing a commotion. She's prone on the floor, her face next to her spilled champagne.

Thomas and I rush to her and help her to her feet.

Her cheeks are crimson. "This is the first and last time I wear heels!"

She takes a step and halts, cringing.

Thomas squats next to her. "Which foot?"

She points at her left leg.

He removes her shoe, takes her foot in his hands and begins to press various parts of it. "Does it hurt here? And here? What about here?"

She shakes her head to each of his questions, gazing at him as if he was an apparition. Next, he palms her ankle and asks her to take another step.

"Sprained but not broken," he declares, standing up.

While he helps her limp toward the nearest chair, I go to the drink table to get her a new glass. When I return with it, Celine and Thomas are sitting next to each other, chatting. Her foot is on his lap.

"It's best to keep it elevated until she gets home and applies ice," he explains.

Celine's expression is dreamy, like she can't believe this is happening to her.

"Do you go to the library often?" she asks him.

He shakes his head.

I bug my eyes at him from behind Celine's back.

"But I love reading," Thomas adds quickly. "I have a big library at home."

I was over at his place in Dijon a few weeks ago. There was no library there, big or small.

You're digging your own grave, man.

"In my Paris apartment," Thomas says.

Oh, I see what he's doing. He's hoping to seduce Celine locally and confine their fling to Burgundy.

That way, she'll never see his Paris apartment and have a chance to call him out.

"Would you like to see it?" he asks her.

Celine tilts her head. "Your library?"

"Yes." He stares into her eyes. "I'll be working from Paris next month, and if you can take a weekend off and visit me, you can borrow as many books as you want."

"Thank you," she says. "I will."

I leave them to their own devices, hoping that Thomas won't wait too long before telling Celine he doesn't read outside of math and finance, and that he's a banker. Scanning the room, I spot Ma who's found Anne-Chantal and a few other cronies.

Good.

Anne-Chantal will give her a lift, which means I can go home now.

The door opens, and before I've even turned to see who it is, I know it's Rissa.

As soon as she spots me, she makes a beeline in my direction. "I was hoping to find you here."

"Aren't you supposed to be packing?" I say. "That is, if you're still leaving the day after tomorrow."

She smiles. "Most of my stuff is already in Paris, and I'll come and get the rest next weekend."

I say nothing. There's nothing to say.

She moves closer. "I've been... thinking about you."

"Of course," I say, expelling a bitter snort. "That's why you called and texted *all the time*."

"Neither did you."

"You're the one who sneaked out in the morning." I give her a hard stare, even as my hands burn to touch her, to press her to my chest. "You're the one who's leaving."

She nods and looks down at her feet. "I wanted to ask a favor."

"Ask."

She probably wants me to keep her boxes until next weekend, seeing as there's plenty of room on the farm.

Her eyes are still downcast as she says, "Will you make love to me tonight, one last time?"

10

CLARISSA

He takes a few endless moments to consider my unorthodox request, and eventually he says yes.

We drive to my spartan apartment in silence.

I hope he'd back me to the wall and kiss me as soon as we get in like when we went to his cottage. Except he doesn't. We stand in my entryway, avoiding each other's eyes.

Nathan presses his mouth into a hard line.

My heart clenches in my chest.

I've grown familiar with this feeling ever since Nathan and I spent that night in the Grotto two weeks ago. Still, it leaves me perplexed. How can a man I barely know suddenly matter so much? Why do I feel so sad leaving him behind? Why do I hunger for him as if he were the only one for me? As if I were in love.

It's perfectly absurd!

Worse, it's ridiculous, shallow, and downright moronic.

Oh, I have tried telling myself it's not him, it's his size.

More exactly, the incredible sensation of being stretched and filled so completely. I've never experienced it before, and I'm unlikely to experience it again.

Perhaps not even tonight, if the way things are going is any indication.

But, deep in my soul, I know it's not just his cock or his lovemaking. It's also the way we connect, the way he makes it easy for me to be candid, to be myself. The way he moves, the way he looks at me. The way everything about him feels right.

Suddenly, a truth I've been choking for days breaks its invisible chains and barrels out. "You're by far the best thing that happened to me since I came to Burgundy."

He says nothing.

"Come away with me," I beg.

"There's nothing for me in Paris."

"Not true! I know a lot of people there, I'll help you find a job, and then—"

He shakes his head.

Oh, Nathan.

I take a step toward him. "Then tonight is all we have."

His gaze sears me.

"Here I am," he says. "Mad at you for leaving, and at the same time, craving you, dying to bury myself in you."

God help me, I'm dying to let you.

"Nathan... I feel empty inside." My voice is hoarse with lust. "Please."

His chest rises and falls and his eyes grow darker.

I take another step and slip a hand under the hem of his sweater, flattening it against his hard stomach.

Suddenly, his hands are everywhere on my body, my face, in my hair. Sweaters are pulled over heads, shirts unbuttoned, and belts hit the carpet with a thump.

I lead him to the bedroom where I remove his underwear. He bares my breasts, sweeping his tongue over my stiff nipples. As he alternates between them, his hand slips inside my panties and I moan at his touch.

Reaching down, I touch him, too.

Ooh, that sweet thickness! It belongs inside me.

"Tell me what you crave," he murmurs. "I want to hear it."

"Your hot skin against mine. You on top of me, around me, in me."

He groans. "Rissa."

I gaze at his massive shaft. Then I kneel and lick the underside, every vein on it, the head and the small slit.

My center throbs, heavy, needy.

Nathan pulls me up. "I want to come when I'm inside you."

"Here, I bought the biggest condoms I could find." I hand him the pack.

He glances at it. "They'll do."

Climbing on the bed, he stretches himself on his back. "Will you try to take me in as deep as you can?"

I nod, removing my panties.

He places his hands on my hips as I settle on his broad tip and begin to lower myself slowly, his expanse stretching me, filling me. With every breath, I impale myself a little more, take a little more of him, almost weeping with the joy of it.

When he's as deep as last time, I pause.

"It's OK, baby, no need to push more." He frowns in concern. "I wouldn't want to hurt you."

"You're not hurting me."

The crease between his brows remains.

"I just stopped so I could feel your shape inside me," I say, rocking my hips, my voice coarse with lust and emotion. "I can take more."

"Rissa—"

"I want to take more."

As I push myself a little more down his throbbing shaft, he cups my mound and begins to stroke. His gaze is a silent plea. Wetness gushes in me, and I open a little wider still, slide down more, caressing him with my inner muscles, until his tip hits my womb. I draw in a breath and bear down a little more, making that contact tighter. There's no more room inside me for him to invade.

"Oh, Rissa," he rasps. "Sweetheart, I'm in to the hilt. So deep."

Lifting his head, Nathan stares at where we're joined. I stare, too, lightheaded, sweat running down my forehead. I wipe it from my left temple.

He reaches up and wipes my forehead and right temple with his big hand. "I've never been so deep in a woman, didn't think it was possible."

His shaft twitches inside me, making my eyes roll in my head.

Through the haze, I hear him say, "Thank you for this gift."

And I fall apart, my legs shaking uncontrollably.

He waits until I've ridden my first orgasm, then lifts me up and lays me on my back. "Want more?"

"Yes."

"Hard?"

"Yes."

Nathan slams into me, making me yelp and cling to him, digging my fingers into his back. He pumps deep and fast, no longer anxious he might hurt me, no longer trying to control himself. I should be wary, but instead I spur him with my heels, urging him to penetrate me deeper. To take everything.

My second orgasm is the most powerful I've ever had. He thrusts relentlessly, and I come and come, crying out his name. His face contorts as he comes, too, his pleasure consuming him.

When he collapses on top of me, I breathe him in, kissing his face and squeezing his tight butt.

"If I didn't know better, I'd say you really liked me," he mutters, pushing my damp hair from my forehead.

"I do."

He pulls back a little and stares into my eyes. "Stay in Burgundy, with me."

"I can't." I hold his gaze. "Come with me to Paris."

He shakes his head.

I almost beg him to at least come visit me occasionally, before I stop myself.

There's too much intensity, too much passion between us. I don't want compromises. If we aren't going to be together fully—body, heart, and soul—then it's best we make a clean cut now and never see each other again.

11

CLARISSA

Yes, I know I said a clean cut.

But that was before I spent a month in Paris—in my favorite season of the year, among new colleagues who turned out to be much kinder than I'd feared—feeling so lonely I cried myself to sleep every night.

It had been a mistake to stay the night at Nathan's cottage. It had been an even bigger mistake to take him to my place in Auxerre. If I count the night in the Grotto, that's three nights we've spent together.

Only three nights, for heaven's sake.

So why do I miss him so much—in my flesh, in my bones, in my soul? Why can't I move on?

"It was nice seeing you again," Nina says, breaking me out of my bleak thoughts. "And thank you for those exquisite chocolates!"

"Oh, it was nothing."

"You kidding? They were delish! Did you see how fast they disappeared? I've noted the name of the shop to be sure I buy some next time I'm in Paris."

"Glad you liked them."

"Will you come down to the Grotto again, or do you have everything you need for your research?" Nina asks.

"I think I'm good, at least for a while."

She nods, her eyes on the road.

"Thanks again for driving me to the train station," I say. "You really didn't have to—I could've called a cab."

She waves dismissively.

"How do you like your new boss?" I ask.

"He's OK... bit boring though. We had more fun when you were around."

I smile. "What about the guy you were dating?"

"Still dating." Her lips twitch at some private thought—no doubt a good one, judging by her smug expression. "It's getting serious."

"Hey, I'm so happy for you!" I pat her shoulder before blurting, "Have you seen Nathan Girault since I left? The farmer I got trapped in the Grotto with..."

Please, keep your eyes on the road, Nina!

I'm blushing so furiously that if she looks at me now, she'll imagine all kinds of crazy things he and I might have done while we were trapped.

And she'd be right.

"I haven't seen him," Nina says. "But Anne-Chantal talks about him sometimes."

Do I have the guts to ask her what exactly Anne-Chantal has said?

Nina glances at me, sympathy in her eyes. "He's been working really hard. And *not* dating anyone."

I turn away and stare out the window.

Three minutes later, she pulls up at the Gare d'Auxerre-Saint-Gervais and I get out. We hug. Nina drives off. I enter the station and find my platform on the flap display. The clock on the wall tells me it's time to go. With a determined nod to no one in particular, I rush to my platform.

"The TGV to Paris leaves in three minutes," a woman announces over the loudspeaker.

I adjust the straps of my backpack, drop my head to my chest in defeat, and march back into the lobby.

This train will leave without me—I'll take the next one in two hours.

My hands are shaking when I pull out my phone and call Nathan, telling myself he might be somewhere with no reception. Or he might not pick up, too busy harvesting or taking care of his cows.

Even if he does answer the phone, there's no reason to expect him to drop everything and drive thirty minutes here and thirty minutes back to his farm just so he can say hi to me. No reason whatsoever. What's going to happen is that I'll eat a solo dinner at the station bistro, check my emails, and take the next train to Paris at eight o'clock.

Forty minutes later, Nathan sits down next to me at a small table on the bistro's terrace.

Clad in worn jeans and a white tee, he looks even brawnier than I remembered. My gaze caresses his body and lingers on his suntanned face.

God, how I've missed him!

We don't say much for the first five minutes.

To calm down, I try to focus on the sounds and smells of the bustling station.

Freshly brewed coffee. Gas. Waiters zooming back and forth, balancing trays.

One of them brings us coffee and iced Perrier.

A chime sounds, followed by the woman on the loudspeaker who delivers the usual security announcement. Travelers rush into the building, gazing up at the displays. Others drag their luggage out and wave to the nearest cabbie.

I have a hard time breathing.

Nathan's left arm and leg are almost touching mine, and his masculine scent makes my head spin, reminding me of our first night in the Grotto. My heartbeat is so wild, I'm not even sure I'm capable of speech right now.

"How's the new job?" Nathan asks.

Inhale. "Fine." *Exhale.* "You?"

"Busy, as usual."

I nod.

We sip our drinks without looking at each other.

Is he over me?

Was he ever into me, to start with?

I sneak a peek at his broad chest. It's heaving. *He's nervous!* Unless, of course, it's normal for a big guy with so much muscle and a strong heart to breathe like that.

My train leaves in less than an hour.

Speak now, Clarissa, or forever hold your peace.

Except, what I intend to say will make me look pathetic—more pathetic than I've ever felt in my life.

I can't say it.

I *won't* say it.

I *am* saying it, because it's my voice that murmurs, "Will you come visit me one of these days?"

He turns toward me and stares.

I hold his gaze.

"Rissa..." He sighs before shaking his head.

I don't like his sighing or his frowning or his shaking his head. I don't like it at all.

"It's been hard forgetting you," he says. "Really, really hard. But I'm working on it."

"I've given up."

He takes my hand and presses it to his lips.

"Please, Nathan, can we give the long-distance thing a shot?"

"The long-distance thing is for college kids." He smirks before adding, "Not that I would know."

"It isn't just for kids!"

"Anyway, I can't. Not with you."

I search his face. "Why not?"

He lets go of my hand and turns away.

"Why not?" I ask again.

"Because..." He turns back to me—his eyes filled with anger and desire and regret. "Because of who I am. Because I'm tied... I'm *married* to the family farm. I'm bound to my land and to the herd."

I chew on my lips as desperation sets in.

"If I start a long-distance relationship with you..." His frown deepens. "Fuck that, if I as much as spend one more night with you, I'll ditch everything and move to Paris."

I swallow. *Yes, please!*

"Do you know how many times I've envisioned that since you left?" His expression is unbearably hard. "And here's what I think would happen. I'd move in with you and become a kept man. I would idle my days away in a city where I don't belong and where my skills are useless. You'd begin to resent me."

"Sounds very... apocalyptic."

He doesn't respond.

I squeeze my eyes shut before opening them. "Fine. Stay here. I'll do the moving."

"What?"

"I'll quit my job and move in with you. I'll do my best to adjust, to help you with the farm, learn your way of life—"

"That's nuts. You can't just—"

"I'm in love with you."

He shuts his mouth.

"I'm in love with you," I say again, my voice cracking.

"You *want* me." He furrows his brow. "It's called lust."

"Oh, I want you all right, but what I feel is so much more!"

"I don't get it." His gaze bores into mine. "I mean, I totally get why you'd *want* me, but not— You called me Cowboy, remember? What would a smart, cultured woman like you find in an uneducated hillbilly?"

I cup his face, shocked by how little he thinks of himself, by how blind he is to his own wondrousness. Should I mention his loyalty first? Or his drive? What about his decency, his kindness, his humor—

Nathan puts his hand over mine and squeezes gently. His eyes are so sad it breaks my heart.

"I'll... draw up... a list," I say through tears.

Pulling me to his chest, he wipes away my tears with the pad of his thumb. "I love you, babe."

I eye his mouth, my heart swelling with hope.

Kiss me.

He kisses my forehead. "You're the most amazing woman I ever met, Rissa, and I sure as hell won't let that woman ruin her life."

NATHAN

S ummer is here, and our cows now spend their days outside, roaming freely and grazing to their hearts' content.

Earlier this week we moved the last calves born in April out of their hutches. In a couple of months, the males will be sold to feedlots, and the females will be raised to become milking cows like their mothers.

Life goes on.

"You're unhappy," Ma says as we clean the barn.

"I'm perfectly satisfied with my existence."

"Oh really?" She tilts her head to the side. "Is that why you never smile anymore?"

I frown. "Yes, I do."

"Nope. You haven't smiled once since your Clarissa left for Paris."

"She was never mine," I say. "And she has nothing to do with this."

We finish in silence and head for the house to have lunch with our volunteers. But before we go in, she stops in her tracks and turns to me.

"What is it, Ma?"

"I want to tell you a story."

"Now? Here?"

She nods. "I've never told you this and it's been gnawing at me."

"OK."

"In your last months of middle school when you told your teachers you were going to continue at an agricultural *lycée*, your father and I received a visit."

"Who?"

"Your principal. She said it would be a waste of talent to send you to a vocational school, that you should be encouraged to go to college and study economics, law, medicine, engineering—anything you wanted—because you had the capacity for it."

"What?"

"She said you had a good head for math. She showed us your grades."

"They were nothing special."

Ma lets out a sigh. "That's what you think because that's what your dad put in your head."

"What are you saying, Ma?" I narrow my eyes. "I know what my grades were. I saw them, remember?"

"Yeah, but you misinterpreted them. Your dad managed to convince you that only straight-A students should go to college. But your grades were solid."

I fold my arms over my chest and stare at her.

"Your principal said, 'Consider this—Nathan gets those grades without even trying. I know he helps you with the farm when he should be doing homework.' "

"What did you say?"

"I wanted to ask her more questions, but your father exploded. He started yelling at the woman."

Ma tries to imitate his voice. "What's wrong that? What's wrong with agriculture and running a dairy farm? How do you think your favorite milk, yogurt, and cheese land on your table? Why the hell is it a waste of talent if Nathan chooses the life of a farmer?"

I find it hard to picture Pop yelling at my school principal like that, and yet I don't doubt for a second that Ma is telling the truth.

She shifts uncomfortably. "Your principal asked if the life of a farmer was what *you* wanted, what *you'd* chosen. Your dad said yes."

"We'd discussed it at some point," I say, jumping to his defense.

"I was there when you did," Ma says. "It wasn't a discussion. It was a monologue. *His.*"

"Why are you telling me this now?"

"To come clean." She gives me a weak smile. "I'm just as much to blame as your dad for robbing you of choices."

I smirk. "So, I should hate both of you now."

"I hope not," she says. "I adore you. So did your dad. He was a good man."

"I know that."

She nods. "I loved him deeply, and he was sick, and I... I refused to see what he was doing to you, how he was undermining your self-confidence."

"Ma—"

"At that age," she interrupts me, "kids aren't supposed to think they have no choice but to honor the decisions that were made for them. They're supposed to think the sky is the limit."

"How do you know I wouldn't have chosen this life anyway even if I was encouraged to look elsewhere?"

"I don't know that," she says. "But what I do know is that keeping the farm in the family was more important to your dad than anything. It was the destiny he'd chosen for himself and for you, and I was too weak to argue."

"Is this about...?" I pause, looking for the right words. "Ma, are you trying to set me free to be with Ri — Clarissa?"

"It's more about... making amends to you, my boy.

And, yes, I'm also trying to set you free to live the life you choose."

I clasp my hands over my head and stare at her for a long moment. "Whatever choice I make, we're not selling the farm."

She raises her eyebrows.

"Because if we do," I say, "Pop's sacrifice would've been for nothing."

EPILOGUE

CLARISSA

I'm in London for the decade's biggest conference on cave art, organized by the Royal Archaeological Society.

If I don't get up, I'll risk being late for my own presentation. Yep, Dr. Penelope Muller Girault is slated to open the conference with a talk on the educational function of upper Paleolithic cave paintings.

Luckily, I don't need to take the Tube to get to the conference held at the British Museum. All I need to do is cross Russell Square.

Problem is, it feels too good to be in bed—and in Nathan's arms.

Around this time three years ago, we walked out of the Darcy Grotto into the sunlight and said goodbye to each other.

I thought that was it.

Boy, was I off the mark.

A lot happened in the months that followed the "cave incident." I moved to Paris and started a new job at the Museum of Archeology. Celine, who's my BFF now, fell madly in love with Nathan's cousin Thomas. I knew he'd felt the same way about her when a week before her first visit, he bought hundreds of books and ditched the home cinema in his Paris apartment to install a wall-to-wall library.

They married five months later.

In July that year, after a cathartic conversation with his mom, Nathan had an epiphany. He realized life didn't have to be black or white. And, as far as his farm was concerned, it didn't have to be all or nothing.

He and Brigitte sold half of their land, which fetched them a small fortune. To increase their profit margin from what was left, they converted his cottage into a second guesthouse and transitioned to organic farming. It was a relatively easy switch, what with the herd being a grazing one to start with.

Nathan hired a manager to help Brigitte operate the farm. He partnered with Thomas, and together they opened a fancy store in Auxerre. The store sells mouthwatering yogurts, cheese, ice cream, and other premium dairy products in funky packaging.

When he called me in September to ask if I was

still interested in him, my "Yes, I am!" tumbled out in a rush of mad joy before he'd finished his question. The truth was, I'd been borderline suicidal all summer, and I was seriously considering an unsolicited relocation to the village of Verlezy. And, possibly, a hunger strike.

Good thing he'd announced he was moving to Paris before I had a chance to say that.

Nathan and Thomas are now proud owners of three Girault's Finest stores in Paris and five in Burgundy. The plan is to expand into Belgium next.

With an effort, I roll off my husband's chest and head to the bathroom. "Call Brigitte!"

"Why, do you doubt my mother's capacity to look after a garden gnome?"

"May I remind you the garden gnome in question is now superfast and primed for mischief?"

"I'll call her," he says.

In fact, I don't doubt Brigitte's skills as a grandmother for a second, but I know how much she enjoys early morning briefings with her son. He enjoys them, too, but he gets sloppy when traveling abroad.

I can't believe it's been three years!

Three years, one kid, seven articles, one monograph, two hundred new cows, eight Girault's Finest stores. And counting.

"What about the Tokyo job offer?" Nathan asks when I come out of the shower.

I glance at my watch, which says I need to be out the door within the next five minutes. "I wrote them yesterday with a 'very honored but can't.' "

"Rissa, you said it was a fantastic opportunity when they'd reached out to you. I don't want you to sacrifice your career—"

"Nobody's sacrificing anything," I declare. "I have an excellent job in Paris. Tokyo will wait."

He draws his eyebrows together in confusion. "Until when?"

"Until you're ready to open stores in Asia."

"You think Thomas and I can pull that off—stores in Asia?" he asks, grinning.

I bend down and kiss the top of his head. "I think the sky is your limit, Cowboy."

AUTHOR'S NOTE

The "twisted feet" that Clarissa discovers on a horse in the Darcy Grotto are a real feature of horses in the Lascaux cave (France). I took a bit of artistic license ascribing this well-known fact and its explanation to my protagonist.

The Darcy Grotto in this book is fictional, but it is inspired by three amazing rock-art caves in France.

My main inspiration is the cave complex near the village of Arcy-sur-Cure in Burgundy. Just like the Darcy Grotto, the real *Grotte d'Arcy* is located on private land, which is currently owned by Gabriel de la Varende. The paintings and engravings in the *Grotte d'Arcy* are "only" 28,000 years old.

My second inspiration is the world-famous Lascaux complex in Dordogne. The age of its spectacular paintings is a measly 18,000 years.

My third inspiration is the Chauvet cave in the Ardèche region whose 32,000-year-old cave art is the most magnificent and oldest in France.

The Chauvet and Lascaux caves have been closed to the public, to protect the art inside from the damaging mold and bacteria caused by thousands of daily visitors. So, what you'll see if you go there will be copies, or *replicas*, not the actual caves.

The Grotte d'Arcy, on the other hand, is still accessible (only until they build a replica, no doubt), so grab your chance to see the real thing while you can!

Thank you for reading **CLARISSA & THE COWBOY**!

If you enjoyed it, please **tell your friends about this book** and consider leaving a short (or long) review on Amazon to help others discover my work.

THANK YOU!

Alix

FREE DOWNLOAD

YOUR FREE E-BOOKS

2 ALIX NICHOLS STORIES
FREE with SIGNUP!

Sign up for my newsletter
by typing this url into your browser:
alixnichols.com/freebie .

You'll be the first to hear about my new releases, book

and gift card giveaways, special offers and reading recommendations.

No spam, ever!

You will also receive
one of my *La Boheme* rom-coms,
You're the One,

and **a newsletter-exclusive *Xereill* novelette**,
A Night of Amity.

If there's one man that store clerk and amateur photographer Diane Petit really, really, actively hates, it's fragrance mogul Sebastian Darcy who stole her father's company--and wrecked the man's health in the process.

But the arrogant SOB had better brace himself because
Diane has vowed revenge.
And revenge she will have.

CHAPTER ONE

I t is a truth universally acknowledged that a young man in possession of a vast fortune must be an entitled SOB born into money. Either that or a rags-to-riches a-hole who bulldozed his way to said fortune, leaving maimed bodies in his wake.

The ferocious-looking PA returns to her desk. "Monsieur Darcy is still in a meeting."

"That's OK." I smile benignly. "I can wait."

I place my hands demurely on my knees and stare at the portrait adorning—or should I say disfiguring—the wall across the hallway from where I'm seated.

Pictured is Count Sebastian d'Arcy du Grand-Thouars de Saint-Maurice, the oldest son of the late Count Thibaud d'Arcy du Grand-Thouars de Saint-Maurice and the inheritor of an estate estimated at around one billion euros. Said estate isn't your run-of-the-mill stock holdings or start-up fortune. Oh no. It's made up of possessions that were handed down—uninterrupted and snowballing—all the way from the Middle Ages.

Even Robespierre and his fellow revolutionaries

didn't get their greedy little hands on the d'Arcy fortune.

What are the odds?

Upon his father's premature demise ten years ago, young Sebastian moved back into the town house in the heart of Le Marais and took the reins of the family's main business. A twenty-three-year-old greenhorn at the time, you'd expect him to make tons of bad decisions and sink the company or, at least, diminish its value.

But no such luck.

Instead, Sebastian Darcy took Parfums d'Arcy from number three to the number one European flavor and fragrance producer—a feat that neither his illustrious grandfather nor his star-crossed father had managed to accomplish.

According to my research, also about ten years ago, the new count chose to go by "Darcy," abandoning the apostrophe and the rest of his status-laden name. I'm sure he only did it to fool those *beneath* him—which includes most everyone in a country that guillotined its royals—into believing that he sees himself as their equal.

The hell he does.

Sebastian Darcy is a stinking-rich aristocrat with instincts of an unscrupulous business shark. This means he qualifies in both the SOB and the a-hole categories.

No, scratch that. He *slays* both categories.

And I hate him more than words can say.

The straitlaced man on the wall seems to smirk. I shudder, my nerves taut to the point of snapping. Will they kick me out if I spit at the photo? Of course they will. I steal a glance at the PA stationed between me and Darcy's office. She looks like a cross between a human and a pit bull. I'm sure she'd love to stick something other than paper between the jaws of her sturdy hole punch.

My hand, for example.

But I didn't come here to fight with Darcy's PA. I'll keep my saliva in my mouth, my eyes cast down, my butt perched on the edge of the designer chair, and my knees drawn together and folded to the side.

Like the meek little mouse I'm trying to pass for.

After waiting three weeks, I'm careful not to arouse any suspicion in Pitbull's mind so she won't cancel my appointment with Darcy.

Eyes on the prize, Diane! Don't forget you're here to declare war by spitting in Count Sebastian Darcy's face, rather than at his photographic representation.

I look at the photo again, arranged in perfect symmetry between the portraits of his grandfather, Bernard, who founded the company, and his father,

Thibaud, who almost put the lid on it. I know this because I've done my homework.

During my week-long research, I dug up every piece of information the Internet had to offer about Sebastian Darcy and his family. I was hoping to find dirt, and I did. The only problem was it was already out in the open—common knowledge, yesterday's news.

And completely useless as leverage.

Pitbull looks up from her smartphone. "Monsieur Darcy is delayed. Do you mind waiting a little longer?"

"No problem." I smile politely. "I'm free this afternoon."

She arches an eyebrow as if having a free afternoon is something reprehensible.

How I wish I could stick out my tongue! But instead I widen my already unnaturally wide smile.

She frowns, clearly not buying it.

I turn away and stare at Darcy's likeness again. In addition to the now-stale scandal, my research has revealed that Darcy is close to his middle brother, Raphael, and also to a longtime friend—Laurent something or other. Our vulture-man even managed to have a serious girlfriend for most of last year. A food-chain heiress, she looked smashing at the various soirées, galas, and fundraisers where she was photographed on his arm. Darcy was rumored to be so into his rich beauty he was about to propose. But then she suddenly dumped him about six months ago.

Clever girl.

He has no right to be happy when Dad's life is in shambles.

I won't stop until I crush him, even if it means I go to jail—or to hell—for using black-hat tactics. It's not as if they'd let me into heaven, anyway. I've already broken the arms and legs on Darcy's voodoo doll.

There's no turning back after you do that sort of thing.

The next step is to let the world know who he really is and hurt him in a variety of ways, big and small. And then, just before delivering the deathblow, let him know he's paying for his sins.

That's why my first move is to show him my face and make sure he remembers it and associates it with *unpleasantness*. That way, when the shit hits the fan, he'll know which creditor is collecting her debt.

Pitbull breaks me out of my dream world. "Monsieur Darcy's meeting is running late."

"That's OK, I can—"

"No," she cuts me off. "There's no point in waiting anymore. As soon as the meeting is over, he'll head to the 9th arrondissement, where he's expected at a private reception."

I stand up.

She glances at my bare ring finger. "Mademoiselle, I can reschedule you for Friday, December twelfth. It's two months away, but that's the only—"

"Thank you, but that won't be necessary," I say.

I know exactly which reception Sebastian Darcy is going to tonight.

∼

Chapter Two
Three months later

"It might snow tonight." Octave holds my coat while I wrap a scarf around my neck. "Will monsieur be taking his supper at home?"

As always, I wince at "monsieur," but I do my best not to show it.

Grandpapa Bernard hired Octave before I was born. Roughly Papa's age and a bear of a man, Octave has worked for my family for thirty-odd years, rising from valet to *majordome*. He's seen Raphael, Noah, and me in all kinds of embarrassing situations young boys tend to get themselves into. I've asked him a thousand times to call me Sebastian.

All in vain.

Octave Rossi claims his respect for my *old* family

name, my *noble* title, and my position in society is too strong for him to drop the "monsieur."

So be it.

"Yes," I say. "But I'll come home late, so please tell Lynette to make something light. And don't stay up for me."

He nods. "*Oui*, monsieur."

Chances are he'll be up until I get home.

Since I moved back into the town house after Papa's passing, Octave has been helpful in a way no one, not even Maman—especially not Maman—has ever been. All the little things, from paying electricity bills and hiring help to undertaking necessary repairs and planning reception menus, are taken care of with remarkable efficiency.

When he offered to assist me with my correspondence, I insisted on doubling his salary. My argument was that he'd be saving me the expense of a second PA for private matters.

He caved in only after I threatened to move out and sell the house.

I trust him more than anyone.

"Morning, Sebastian! To the office?" my chauffeur, Greg, asks.

He, at least, doesn't have a problem calling me by my first name.

"We'll make a detour," I say as I climb into the Toyota Prius. "I need to see someone first."

I give him the address, and he drives me to the Franprix on rue de la Chapelle in the 18th arrondissement. Greg parks the car, and I march into the supermarket, scanning the cashiers' counters lined parallel to the shop windows.

There she is!

Diane Petit smiles at a customer as she hands her a bag of groceries. She'll be finishing her shift in about ten minutes, according to the private eye I hired to locate and tail her. I'll talk to her then.

Right now, I pretend to study the selection of batteries and gift cards on display not far from her desk. What I'm really doing is furtively surveying the firebrand who smashed a cream cake in my face in front of a few dozen people last October. At the time, the only thing I registered about her through my surprise and anger was *foxy*.

I've had ample opportunity to pour over her pretty face and eye-pleasing shape in the numerous close-ups the PI has supplied over the past few weeks. I've studied Diane in all kinds of situations and circumstances—at work with her customers, hanging out with her friends, and roaming the streets with her camera, immortalizing everyday scenes of Parisian life. She's hot, all right, but there's also something endearing about her, something unsophisticated and very un-Parisian.

In spite of her extravagant outburst at Jeanne's bash, Diane Petit seems to be an unpretentious small-town bumpkin through and through.

I've learned a good deal about her since that memorable evening. I know she works part time at this supermarket, lives in a high-rise in the 14th, and hangs out with her foster sister Chloe, a coworker named Elorie, and a waitress named Manon.

She enjoys photographing random things, going to the movies, eating chocolate, and drinking cappuccino.

More importantly, I know why Diane did what she did that night at *La Bohème*.

And I plan to use it to my advantage.

Someone gives me a sharp prod in the back.

"Why are you here?" Diane asks as I spin around.

"To give you a chance to apologize."

She smirks. "You're wasting your time."

"No apology, then?"

"You're here to let me know you're on to me, right?" She puffs out her chest. "Read my lips—I'm not afraid of you."

"That's not why I'm here."

"How did you find me, anyway?"

"I hired a professional who tracked you down within days."

She tilts her head to the side. "And you've waited three months before confronting me. Why?"

"I wanted to know what your deal was, so I gave my PI the time to compile a solid profile." I hesitate before adding, "Besides, your foster sister was shot, and you were busy looking after her. I wanted to wait until Chloe had fully recovered."

"You've met Chloe?" She sounds surprised.

"Of course." I shrug. "Jeanne introduced us."

She blows out her cheeks. "What do you want, Darcy?"

"Just to talk."

"About what?"

"I have a proposition that might interest you."

She looks me over. "Unless your proposition is to give me a magic wand that would turn you into a piglet, I'm not interested."

"I obviously can't do that, but what I can do is—"

"Hey, Elorie, are we still on?" Diane calls to a fellow cashier who passes by.

Elorie smiles. "Only if you and Manon let me choose the movie."

"Fine with me, but I can't vouch for Manon."

While Diane and Elorie discuss the time and place of their outing, I resolve to draw Diane somewhere else before making my offer. Preferably, somewhere that's on my turf rather than hers.

"Can we go someplace quieter?" I ask Diane after Elorie leaves.

She sighs. "OK, but don't take it as a good sign."

"Understood."

I do take it as a step in the right direction, though.

She follows me outside and into the car.

"To Le Big Ben, please," I say to Greg.

He nods, and thirty minutes later, Diane and I are seated in a private booth at my favorite Parisian gentlemen's club, which I also happen to co-own with Raphael as of three weeks ago. We've kept the old manager, who's doing an admirable job. I've continued coming here with Laurent or Raph, as a longtime patron who enjoys the subdued elegance of this place and its unparalleled selection of whiskeys. The staff may not even realize the club has changed hands. It's easier this way—and it removes the need for socializing with them.

"So," Diane says after the server brings my espresso and her cappuccino. "What's your proposition?"

"Marry me."

She blinks and bursts out laughing as if I just said something outrageous. Which I guess it was without prior explanation.

Maybe I should start over.

"Here's the deal," I say. "You and I will *date* through April." I make air quotes when I say "date."

She looks at me as if I've lost my mind.

"You'll *move in* with me in May," I continue. "About a month after that, we'll get *married*."

Diane makes a circular motion with her index at the side of her head and mouths, "Nutcase."

"A month into our marriage, I'll *cheat* on you," I continue, undeterred, with a quote unquote on *cheat*. "And then you'll *leave* me."

She gives me a long stare. "Why?"

"It doesn't concern you. What you need to know is that I'm prepared to pay fifty thousand euros for a maximum of six months in a pretend relationship."

"Why?" she asks again.

"You don't need to know that."

"OK, let me ask you something I do need to know." She arches an eyebrow. "Why *me*?"

I shrug.

"If you continue ignoring my legitimate questions," she says, "I'm out of here before you finish your espresso."

"You're perfect for a plan I'd like to set in motion," I say. "And as an incentive for you to play your role the best you can, I'll quadruple your fee if my plan succeeds."

"How will I know if it succeeds if you won't even tell me what it is?"

"Trust me, you'll know." I smirk. "Everyone in my entourage will."

Diane leans back with her arms crossed over her chest. "Can't you find another candidate for your shady scheme? It couldn't have escaped your notice that I humiliated you in public."

"I assure you it didn't," I say. "But what's really important and valuable here is that it didn't escape other people's notice, either. A picture of my cream-cake-covered mug even ended up in a tabloid or two."

She gives me a smug smile.

"At the time, I told everyone I didn't know you, but I can easily change my tune and *confess* we'd been dating."

"This doesn't make any sense."

"Believe me, it does—a whole lot of sense—if you consider it in light of my scheme."

"Which I can't do," she cuts in, "because you won't tell me what your scheme is."

True. "Anyway, I'll tell everyone we've talked it over and made up."

She says nothing.

"Mademoiselle Petit... Diane." I lean in. "Your parents—and yourself—are *not* in the best financial shape right now. I'm offering an easy solution to your woes."

"Ha!" she interjects with an angry gleam in her

almond-shaped eyes. "Says the person who caused our woes!"

She's right, of course, but not entirely. Before going in for the kill, I did offer to buy out her father's fragrance company. The offer wasn't generous by any measure, but it was reasonable given the circumstances. Charles Petit's artisanal workshop wasn't doing terribly well. In fact, it was of little interest to me, with the exception of the two or three of his signature fragrances that were worth the price I'd offered. Charles is a lousy businessman—but he's a true artist. He *created* the fragrances he sold, and he also created for others. I would've offered him a job in one of my labs had I not been one hundred percent sure he'd decline it.

As it happened, he also declined my fifty thousand, calling me a scumbag and a few other choice epithets I won't repeat in front of a lady. Fifty thousand euros isn't a fortune, but seeing as he stood no chance against me, he should've taken the money.

It was better than nothing.

But Charles Petit proved to be more emotional than rational about his business. And he ended up with nothing. Worse than nothing, actually. I heard he took to drinking, got kicked out by his wife, and had a heart attack. Or was it a stroke?

Anyway, my point is, at least some of those

misfortunes could've been avoided had he sold his company to me.

I open my mouth to say this to Diane, but then it occurs to me she must already know about my offer. She probably also shares Monsieur Petit's opinion that it was indecently low.

"Can we skip the whole dating and marrying nonsense," Diane says, "and go straight to the part where you grovel at my dad's feet, thrust a check for two hundred thousand into his hand, and beg him to take it in the hopes he might forgive you one day?"

I sigh and shake my head.

She stands. "The answer is no."

"Why don't you think it over? I'll be in touch next week." I set a twenty on the table. "May I offer you a ride?"

"Thank you, Monsieur Darcy, you're very *kind*." She bares her teeth in a smile that doesn't even try to pass for a real one. "But I prefer the *métro*."

Chapter Three

"Will you remind me again why we're on a *bus* just before the rush hour?" Elorie gives me a sour look, hugging her counterfeit Chanel bag to her chest.

I admit, it was a mistake. But I'm not admitting this out loud.

"It takes us straight to the bistro I've been telling you about," I say. "Like a taxi."

Elorie snorts. "Taxi, my foot! When I take a cab, I sprawl comfortably and give this baby"—she points at her bag—"its own seat. Whereas now—"

She jostles the woman on her left. "Madame, you're stepping on my foot!"

The woman apologizes and shifts a couple of inches, which is no mean feat, considering how packed the bus is.

Elorie turns back to me. "You said the bistro was in the 9th, yes?"

I nod.

"At this rate, it'll take us an hour to get there."

I'm about to suggest we get off and find the nearest *métro* station when two school kids jump out of their seats and make their way to the exit.

We take their seats immediately.

"Ah," Elorie says. "This is better. Not a taxi by a long shot, but still."

We're on this bus because I'm taking Elorie to celebrate at *La Bohème*, my favorite bistro in Paris. Perhaps even more than its amazing cappuccinos and out-of-this-world chocolate mousse, I love that bistro because it's home to two terrific chicks—Manon and

Jeanne. Headwaiter Manon is my gym and movies companion, and she's the sweetest person I've ever met. Proprietor Jeanne's personality is so mood enhancing she should charge a supplement every time she tends the bar. Jeanne also happens to have a brother, Hugo, who happens to be my sister Chloe's fiancé. In other words, she's almost family.

How cool is that?

Regardless, I'd half expected her to declare me persona non grata for crashing her latest reception and assaulting one of her guests. The guest in question—Sebastian Darcy—is her husband's friend and political backer, which makes my smashing a cream cake in his face an even bigger affront. But Jeanne just laughed the incident off, saying the bash had been too stuffy and in serious need of an icebreaker.

Which I kindly provided.

The Manon-Jeanne combo makes me feel truly welcome at *La Bohème*. So much so that I forget I'm far away from home in a metropolis of eleven million people, suburbs included. The vast majority of them are crammed into tiny apartments and deeply convinced they're the most evolved representatives of the human race. Here in Paris, if you say *bonjour* to a stranger on the street, they think you're either a nutcase or a hooker.

"How's *the quest* coming along?" I ask Elorie.

The quest is shorthand for Elorie's newfound mission—locate an eligible billionaire and get him to marry her. Elorie defines "eligible" as currently available, reasonably young, and passably good-looking.

She launched the project three months ago on her twenty-sixth birthday, and she's been working hard on it ever since. Not very successfully, judging by the sound of it. But what's three months when looking for a soul mate who meets such high standards and such specific... specifications?

"I've made good progress," Elorie says.

I bug out my eyes. "I want a name!"

"Not so fast, *ma cocotte*. My progress is theoretical at this point."

"Oh."

"Don't you *oh* me." Elorie wags her index finger from side to side. "Would you launch a business without conducting a market study first?"

"I guess not." I narrow my eyes. "Do you approach all your dreams as a business?"

She shrugs. "Not all—only the ones worth pursuing. Anyway, as the saying goes, if you practice without theory, you shall fall into the ditch."

"There's no such saying."

"You sure?" She puts her chin up. "Well, there should be. Anyway, I stand on much firmer ground today than three months ago all because I've done enough research to write a thesis on the topic."

"Maybe you should write one," I mutter.

Elorie is the most entertaining person I've ever met and I love her, but her pragmatism does rattle me sometimes. Then again, I'm well aware I'm a country-fried prawn who still hasn't wrapped her head around big-city attitudes.

"Ha-ha, very funny!" Elorie pauses before adding, "Anyway, I've now read all the tutorials and how-to articles I could get my hands on, and I've analyzed several real-life case studies."

"I'm impressed."

"Me, too," she says with a wink. "I've never taken anything so seriously in my whole life."

"*Mesdames*, *messieurs*," the bus driver says into the speaker. "This bus will not continue beyond Opéra. You can wait for the next one or take an alternate route."

People gripe and boo and begin to move toward the doors.

I spread my arms in apology.

Elorie rolls her eyes.

We get off and continue our journey using the most reliable means of transportation in Paris—our feet. The air is cold and humid, which is no surprise in February, but at least it isn't raining.

I look up at the leaden sky and tone down my gratitude—it isn't raining *yet*.

"Feel like sharing your theoretical findings?" I ask, tucking my scarf inside my coat in an attempt to shield myself from the cutting wind.

Elorie considers my request. "OK. But only because you're my friend and you always pay for the drinks."

"Aww." I place my hand on my heart. "You put 'friend' before 'drinks,' you wonderful person."

"Listen up—because I won't repeat this," Elorie says, choosing to ignore my irony. "The single most important action you can take is to hang out where billionaires do."

"In Swiss banks?"

"For example." She nods, unfazed. "Don't tell me you believe Kate would've snatched William if her clever mom hadn't sent her to the University of St Andrews, where the cream of British nobility goes?"

"I must confess I haven't given the matter much thought."

"Then thank me for opening your eyes."

"Thank you," I say dutifully. "But we have a problem—I'm too old for college, and it isn't my thing, anyway."

"That's OK," she says. "It was just an example."

"Phew." I'm doing my best to keep my expression earnest. "What a load off!"

She glances at me sideways and shakes her head. "What I'm telling you isn't funny, Diane. It's precious. I'd be taking notes if I were you."

"Sorry, sweetie. Go on."

"I'll give you a few pointers," she says. "Go horseback riding, join a golf club, or book yourself into a high-end ski resort. If you're targeting a specific man, go exactly where he goes."

"Some people would call it stalking."

"*I* call it lending fate a hand."

"OK," I say. "What about the rich perverts who frequent BDSM clubs? Should I get a membership for one? And what about the polygamists who make their wives wear burkas? Where do you draw the line?"

"Where he buys me Louboutin pumps, Prada sunglasses, and Chanel purses to wear with my burka." She arches an eyebrow. "If I can travel the world in his private jet and have my own wing in his palace plus three or four maids at my beck and call, then sure, why not. Bring on the burka."

I stop and put my hands on my hips.

Elorie stops, too.

"Aren't you a little too cavalier about this?" My voice betrays my feelings—equal parts incredulity and concern. "Let me be more specific. We're not talking a *burkini* here. We're talking the works with gloves and an eye grid. And *other* wives."

Elorie tilts her head to the side, thinking. "Ten maids, my own palace, and my own jet."

I'm too dumbfounded to speak.

"What?" she says. "Don't look at me like that. Everyone has a price, and so do you."

"I don't think so."

"Of course, you do. You're just too ashamed to admit it, which is kind of sad."

Does she really think that?

"Or maybe you're fooling yourself that your affections can't be bought," she says, her expression pensive. "Which is even sadder."

"Please, believe me when I say I don't care about money." I stare her in the eye. "I don't mind having some—just enough to get by—but I wouldn't make the slightest sacrifice just so I can marry a rich man."

Elorie rolls her eyes, clearly not buying it.

"If you want to know the truth," I say, "I find rich men repulsive. They're so full of themselves, so convinced of their superiority! They gross me out."

"What, all of them?" she asks, raising an eyebrow.

"Without exception. They mistake their dumb luck for divine providence and their lack of scruples for business acumen."

Elorie narrows her eyes. "It sounds like you're

talking about one rich man in particular. And I think it's Sebastian Darcy."

The moment she mentions his name, I realize I've spent the past few weeks doing exactly what Elorie just advised me to do—researching a rich man. But there's a difference. I haven't been investigating him for a chance to marry him. I've been probing into his life in the hopes of finding a weapon to destroy him.

I didn't find any.

And then, three days ago, he showed up at my workplace and handed me one.

Sure, what he's offered is a stick rather than a hatchet. But it's up to me to take that stick and sharpen it into a spear. Our ancestors killed mammoths with spears—I should be able to skewer a man.

"He's superhot, by the way," Elorie says. "I'd marry him even if he was a mere millionaire."

"He's a jerk."

"Who isn't?"

I start walking again. "So you meet the billionaire of your dreams, then what?"

"Duh." She rolls her eyes. "Then I make him fall madly in love with me."

"Of course! How?"

"By being gorgeous, self-confident, and classy."

I clear my throat audibly.

"What was that supposed to mean?" she asks, turning to me.

"We're cashiers." I give her a hard stare. "We may be called *cute* but *gorgeous* and *classy are* beyond our reach."

I expect her to object that you can be classy on a budget, but instead she puts her arm around my shoulders and gives a gentle squeeze.

"Finally," she says with an approving smile. "Diane Petit has demonstrated there's a realist hiding in there, underneath her *principles* and other bullshit."

Her words sting a little.

"My dear," Elorie says as we turn onto rue Cadet. "I'll reward your bout of honesty by giving you the single most precious piece of advice anyone has ever given you. Or ever will."

I halt again and fold my hands across my chest. "I'm all ears."

"I'm sharing this," Elorie says, "because we're besties and because I want you to owe me one."

I shake my head. "You can't link those two reasons with an *and*. They're mutually exclusive. It's either because we're besties *or* because you want me to owe you one."

She sucks on her teeth for a brief moment. "I want you to owe me one."

"OK, what's your precious advice?"

"It's a shortcut that very few women are aware of."

"Yeees?"

"You need to develop a real interest and a certain level of competence in what the billionaires you're targeting are passionate about."

I pull a face. "Things like football?"

"If that's what floats his boat."

"I see."

"It can be all sorts of things." Elorie begins to count on her fingers. "Sports cars. War movies. Guns. High tech gadgets. Video games."

"I think they're a waste of time," I say.

"It doesn't matter what you think. What matters is what you say." She moves on to her right hand. "Mixed martial arts. Wine. Politics. Porn. Art photography."

My eyebrows shoot up.

She giggles. "That last one was a mole to check if you were paying attention. Nobody—except you, that is—cares about art photography."

"I know men who do."

"Are they filthy rich?"

I shake my head.

"Ha! Thought so."

We reach *La Bohème*, and I stop in front of the entrance, pulling Elorie by her sleeve to stop her from walking on.

"OK," I say. "Let's finish this conversation before

we go in. Let's say you've become a wine connoisseur or a sports car buff. How does that guarantee your billionaire will fall to your feet like an electrocuted wasp?"

"It's science, dum-dum." She cocks her head. "Say your man loves Star Wars and football. You give him a well-timed Yoda quote, and his mind goes, 'Ooh, she's special.' Then you give him an analysis of the latest Paris Saint-Germain victory, and his body releases even more happiness hormones. And before he knows it, his brain learns to associate that euphoric state with you. This leads him to conclude you're Mademoiselle Right, which, in turn, leads him to propose."

"Neat," I say.

And what about the billionaire who proposes not because he gives a shit if you're Mademoiselle Right or Mademoiselle One Night, but because he wants to use you in some shady scheme?

I push open the door to the bistro and decide to keep that last observation to myself.

Chapter Four

"So what are we celebrating?" Elorie asks after

we settle at the bar and Manon hands us two tall glasses of *vin chaud*.

The steaming mulled wine smells of cinnamon and orange. It makes my frozen insides relax with comfort and my brain thaw with a pleasant mist in a way that's satisfying beyond words.

Who needs orgasms when you can just take a walk out in the cold and drink this ambrosia?

I grab the spoon in my glass and pull out the half slice of orange begging to be eaten. "Have you heard of *Voilà Paris*?"

"The gossip magazine?"

"They call themselves a women's magazine, but yes, gossip is their main stock in trade." I bite into my orange slice. "They bought some of my pics last month, and now they're hiring me on as a freelance photojournalist."

Elorie frowns. "You're going to be a paparazzo."

I shake my head, unable to speak because of the wine in my mouth.

"They publish articles, too, not just celebrity gossip," Manon says.

I swallow the wine. "The deal is if I produce fun pictures with original captions, they'll let me put them together into a story."

"Congratulations, Diane!" Manon high-fives me and jogs away to take care of other customers.

"Yeah, congrats," Elorie says with a lot less enthusiasm. "Does this mean you'll resign from the supermarket?"

"I can't. Freelancing pays for movie tickets and drinks, but there's also the little matter of rent."

Elorie nods, perking up.

We hang out at *La Bohème* for another hour and then head home. Elorie catches an RER train to her parents' suburban cottage, and I take the *métro* to Chloe's apartment in the 14th. In fact, I should stop thinking of it as Chloe's. Now that she's moved in with Hugo and I've taken over the lease, the place is officially mine.

The next morning, I wake up with a headache that's too strong for the two glasses of mulled wine I had last night. Then I remember I hardly slept, weighing the pros and cons with regards to Darcy's offer just as I'd done the night before and the night before that.

I pop an aspirin and head to the shower.

Darcy's proposition has been on my mind nonstop for three days now. No matter how I turn it, taking him up on his offer is a no-brainer. Basically, there are only two ways this can go. Option A, I play his game and pocket the funds for Dad. Option B, I pretend to play his game, but in reality, I seize the opportunity to poke around his house and dig up some dirt on him. Once I have the info and the evidence, I'll get it published in *Voilà Paris* or leak it to a more serious periodical, depending on the nature of the scoop. This will, hopefully, do some serious damage to Darcy's finances or, at least, tarnish his reputation.

Maybe both. And thus avenge Dad.

My brain prefers Option A, while my gut craves Option B. But here's the best part—I win, no matter how the dice roll, and Dad gets either money or satisfaction. Or both, if I can find dirt and be patient enough to hold onto it until after I am paid. That would make me a villain, and a nasty piece of work, but who says being ruthless is men's prerogative?

Sebastian Darcy is a vulture. He deserves a taste of his own cruelty.

It's in that crucial instant, right after I've shampooed my hair and just before I rinse it, that I decide I'll marry him.

WE MEET in his office because Darcy's schedule for today has only one thirty-minute slot that could be freed.

"I'm glad you were able to see that my offer represents a unique opportunity for you and your family," he says, motioning me to the *informal* area of his ginormous office with comfy leather armchairs and a designer coffee table.

His arrogance is unbearable, but I hold my tongue. If I want my plan to succeed, I need him to trust me.

Pitbull enters with a tray loaded with drinks, pretty little sandwiches, and mouthwatering pastries. She gives me a perplexed look, which tells me she remembers me from my cancelled appointment back in October and wonders if she's pegged me right.

"Could you maybe clue me in on the whys of your offer?" Rather than sitting down, I go to the floor-to-ceiling window and take in the breathtaking view. "It would help to know what I'm getting myself into."

"I explained last time," he says. "And I can assure you it's not illegal or dangerous."

I turn around and give him a stare. "You didn't explain anything. You just said 'I need you to be my pretend girlfriend for a couple of months and then my pretend wife for another month or so.'"

"And that's as much as you need to know," he says, his voice dry. "Take it or leave it."

Fine. Don't tell me. I'll find out on my own.

"Will you please sit down?" He points to the sofa. "I'd like you to look at the contract."

Ah, so there's a written contract. Well, what did I expect?

I amble over to one of the armchairs, plonk myself

down, and pick up an éclair. "I'm not going to sign your contract right away."

"I don't expect you to." He sits down opposite me. "You can study it tonight and call me tomorrow morning, but you can't discuss it with anyone. That's why you'll need to sign *this* before you can see the contract."

He nudges a sheet of paper across the coffee table. The title at the top of the page says, "Nondisclosure Agreement."

How clever of him.

I read and sign the agreement while Darcy wolfs down a few sandwiches, explaining he hasn't had time to eat yet.

Who knew billionaires were such busy people?

"We'll use your dramatic appearance at Jeanne and Mat's party to our best advantage," he says, wiping his fingers with a napkin.

"How?"

"I'll tell everyone we'd been seeing each other discreetly for a few months until you were led to believe I'd cheated on you. But now the misunderstanding is cleared up and we're back together, madly in love."

I narrow my eyes. "Why go out of your way to give a reason for what I did when you can just fall *madly in love* with a fresh face who won't require any explaining."

"Because what you did suggests you're the kind of woman who doesn't put up with cheating."

"And that's good becaaaause…?"

"I can't tell you, but trust me, it's good. In fact, it's perfect for my plan."

I sigh. "Whatever you say."

"Let's look at the contract now, shall we?" He glances at his watch. "My meeting starts in fifteen minutes."

I open the manila folder and stare at the document inside it.

"Most of it is legalese that we can go over next time once we agree on the terms," Darcy says.

I nod.

"You can go straight to this part." He turns several pages and points at a paragraph with bullet points. "Please read this and let me know if you have questions. Or, if you prefer, I can just walk you through it."

I scoff at him. "Coming from a family that's been sending its children to private schools for generations, you may not be aware that France has had free universal education since the 1880s."

He blinks, clearly taken aback. "I'm sorry. I didn't mean to offend you."

"No, it's me who's sorry to shatter your aristocratic illusions," I say. "But cashiers can read."

"I was just trying to be helpful," he says.

I know he is. And it aggravates me. I'd be much more comfortable with him if he'd stop hiding his ugly face behind this mask of polite concern.

Darcy looks at his watch again and taps his index finger on the highlighted passage. "Read this at home, then reread it, and write down all your questions. I'll call you tomorrow night."

Aha, now he's showing his bossy side.

I'm so intimidated.

Not.

"*Oui*, monsieur." I bow my head with exaggerated obedience, noting in passing that Darcy has handsome hands—lean wrists, large palms, and long fingers.

At least the right one, which is currently pinning the contract to the table.

Let's hope his left hand is teeny-weeny. Or super fat. Or excessively hairy.

He doesn't deserve two handsome hands.

"The gist of this paragraph," Darcy says, "is that you recognize you're entering a financially compensated transaction with me, which is couched as a relationship, but is *not* a relationship, be it physical or emotional."

A relationship with an a-hole.

God forbid.

"Consider it recognized," I say.

"It also says here somewhere..." He slides his finger along the lines and halts on one of the bullet points. "Here—it says you commit to moving in with me at about the two-month mark on our timeline."

"Do I have to?"

"This has to be credible for it to work." He makes a sweeping gesture with his other hand, which, unfortunately, is as nicely shaped as the first. "A month after that, I'll propose, and another month after that, we'll marry."

"It'll look rushed. Besides, how are you going to stage a town hall ceremony and—"

"I won't have to. We'll fly to the Bahamas for a week and get *married* there." He uses air quotes.

"Wow, you've thought this through."

"I have, indeed." He clears his throat. "As you can see, the bullet point just below states that sex is not a requirement but you *will* need to touch and kiss me in public."

"Good."

He raises his eyebrows in surprise.

Crap. That came out all wrong.

"What I meant was it's good that sex isn't required. It would've been a deal-breaker."

He nods. "That's what I thought."

"Do I *have* to kiss you?"

"Yes. It doesn't have to be torrid. But if we never kiss, our relationship won't look convincing."

"OK, if we must." I sigh. "So we date, move in together, and smooch on camera. Then what?"

"Then we wait for... a certain person to make his move."

"How very enigmatic." I roll my eyes. "You do realize I'm going to hate every moment of our time together, right?"

"You won't be the only one," he says. "In any event, if nothing happens within six months, we'll break up and I'll pay you for your time. But if my plan works, you'll walk away a rich woman."

Or if *my* plan works, you'll be left a ruined man.

END OF EXCERPT

CONTEMPORARY ROMANCES

La Bohème

You're the One (companion novella)

Winter's Gift

What If It's Love?

Falling for Emma

Under My Skin

Amanda's Guide to Love

The Devil's Own Chloe

The Darcy Brothers

Find You in Paris

Raphael's Fling

The Perfect Catch

Clarissa and the Cowboy (companion novella)

Playing to Win

Playing with Fire

Playing for Keeps

Playing Dirty

SCIENCE FICTION ROMANCES

Keepers of Xereill

The Cyborg's Lady (prequel novella)

The Traitor's Bride

The Commander's Captive

The Dragon's Woman

ABOUT THE AUTHOR

Alix Nichols is an unapologetic caffeine addict and a longtime fan of Mr. Darcy, especially in his Colin Firth incarnation.

She is a USA Today bestselling and Kindle Scout winning author of sexy romances which will "keep you hanging off the edge of your seat" (RT Book Reviews) and "deliver pure pleasure" (Kirkus Reviews).

At the age of six, she released her first romance. It featured highly creative spelling on a dozen pages stitched together and bound in velvet paper.

Decades later, she still writes. Her spelling has improved (somewhat), and her books have topped the Amazon charts around the world. She lives in France with her family and their almost-human dog.

Connect with her online:
Website: http://www.alixnichols.com
Facebook: www.facebook.com/AuthorAlixNichols
Pinterest: http://www.pinterest.com/AuthorANichols
Goodreads: goodreads.com/alixnichols
Twitter: twitter.com/aalix_nichols

43124850R00099